Another Santana Morning

LASTIC PRESS

This first edition of
"Another Santana Morning"
is limited to twenty-six
signed and lettered copies.

This is copy "S"

Mike Dolan

Another Santana Morning

stories

Mike Dolan

LASTIC
PRESS

ISBN number: 978-0-9553181-5-3

Printed and Bound by Biddles, King's Lynn, Norfolk

Cover design and layout by Dean Harkness
(based on an original painting by Bill Hughes)
Typeset by Andrew Hook

Published by:
Elastic Press
85 Gertrude Road
Norwich
UK

elasticpress@elasticpress.com
www.elasticpress.com

This book is dedicated to:

Brian Grainger (Milieu), for kick-starting my previously dead career
back to life,

and to:

Andrew Hook at Elastic Press, for taking up this project despite its
many previous flaws, and running with it,

and, finally, to:

Chaz Brenchley for his fabulous Introduction.

How wonderful it is to know one has these newfound friends!

Table of contents

Time, Considered as a Helix of Semi-Precious Stories

An Introduction by Chaz Brenchley

There is something happily appropriate about a science fiction writer's work being published out of its proper time. It tells us from the start that we are dealing with an imagination set aslant to the common world, with sideslip texts and manifest uncertainties.

Of course, it would be happier still if this book were being published a generation before the stories were written, rather than (as it is) a generation after. If that were so, though, we would be trapped in a metafiction. Which would be interesting – and, again, appropriate – but probably less comfortable than where we are, caught in an exposé of the realities of SF publishing, then and now. The True Confession of *Santana Morning*'s sorry history may be found in the author's own Afterward, but there's a reason why that is set at the end of the book and this introduction at the beginning. That is about the business of publishing; this is about story. Start here.

Short stories are the engine that drives genre. Or you could make that an eco-metaphor, say they are the biological engine that keeps invention fresh. Short stories hurl out the questions that novels seek to answer; in genre terms, it's the short fiction that demands to know "what if?" where the novel seeks out time and space to explore what would happen if. If that makes short stories sound like insistent children who are always asking why, while their adults have to stretch in a vain attempt to satisfy them - well, yes. That may indeed be how I see the relationship.

Put it another way, short stories define the space that novels set out to fill. Certainly for me – and for many other writers I've talked to – it was short stories that laid out the parameters of my imaginative space, both as a reader and a writer. I was a greedy reader, seizing everything that I could lay my hands on, magazines and books and cereal packets; looking back, it was always the short stuff that punched a way through into new territories.

Often and often, it was short stuff like these stories of Mike Dolan's. He and I all too obviously read the same authors; he was a decade or so ahead of me – his 1960s were my 1970s, essentially – or we might have found ourselves trying to write the same stories too, with that same eager adolescent optimism. We didn't all get Ray Bradbury for a mentor (in which Chaz greens with envy...), but much else is familiar, both in the history and in the fiction.

These stories inhabit other worlds, other times, other and alien lives – which is why they seem so familiar, because those are the territories of my own early imagination, as mapped out by other writers much like Dolan: those writers who looked more to the inside, whose stories turned on a human truth more often than an alien invention. It's almost a surprise to understand that I haven't read some of these before, they seem so core to the genre and to my own development.

These are a young man's stories, fresh and untried and interrogative. Also, they date from when the genre itself was still young: before the founding fathers could call themselves grandfathers, as it were. They don't all work, perhaps, on their own terms; some of them don't necessarily work on our terms, because both the genre and its readership have grown more sophisticated in the intervening years. No matter. If anything, that works to their advantage: the occasional failure serving as a reminder that they come to us from another time, as alien to us now as any world of the imagination.

Dolan says that this is a book about love, and he's not wrong. It's also a book about story – the first and the last stories here are explicit: the one about storytelling, the other about writing – and both of those themes mean that it is a book sometimes about beginnings, sometimes about endings, mostly about those awkward times between the two where something is on the rise, something else on the fall. Love and death and what happens in between: this is the span of life, which means it is the span of literary investigation, and also of a young man's curiosity. Story embraces it all.

Chaz Brenchley
December 2007

Foreword

This is a book about magic. It is also about love…and other emotions. But mainly it concerns those moments when suddenly we become aware of the magical aspects of the world, when we catch a glimpse of reality's other side, peering through ordinary barriers, past a split in the sky, into somewhere else, where we might find something wondrous.

At least, the stories in this book are *attempts* to penetrate these barriers of the mundane, the everyday, the familiar. If a few come close to succeeding, that can be regarded as success indeed. Because boredom is powerful, ruts are easy to follow, and over a period of decades blinders can become not only necessary, but comfortable.

Most of us, in fact, would rather *not* find ourselves turning an odd corner during that halfway time between sunset and the night, when the light is different, to walk into another life. We do not like to have our boats rocked while we're out in the middle of a lake that is far too large and unfriendly, on our separate voyages from birth to death, between the what-is and the what-might-be.

If we see strange swimmers in the water underneath us, or if we throw in our bait and bring up weird-colored fish from a distant planet, we tend to turn the other way and row a little faster. If we turn that corner in the lavender half-light, when there aren't any bright spots or shadows with sharp edges that we can count on, and come face to face with our dreams, we feel an icy chill, our tongues sticking in our throats.

What sustains us at these moments can be defined easily: love.

1

Our emotions betray us.

The most callous among us is vulnerable. We are, after all, members of the animal realm. The faintly salty water of the ancient oceans still flows in our veins. And animals are emotional creatures.

There are negative emotions, such as greed, lust, hatred, envy, fear, and rage. We inherited these to keep us alive in a world filled with teeth and claws, where, on moonless nights, things once moved about in the spreading shadows, beyond the perimeter of the campfire, searching to satisfy their appetite.

But then there are positive emotions too, the chief of which is love. Love can be a need, as well as a fulfillment. Most of the time love is simply there, taken for granted, a half-heard melody threading through our days, a feeling to be appreciated the way one might appreciate a warm room and a soft bed. At other times, and for other people, love is hot and sharp, a crescendo. It grabs us and carries us aloft, into a clear, bright sky, where we can see into the distance, all the way to the farthest horizons.

Along with love come its allied emotions...trust, tenderness, joy, loyalty, forgiveness. If fear closes our eyes and our hearts, love opens them. Details leap out at us with unexpected brilliance. Our minds are flooded with color. Our other senses become more acute as well, so that we taste more intensely, smell subtler fragrances, touch striking new textures, and hear beyond the previous limits of our hearing.

When you love, when you care, when you suddenly become aware of that secret connection, that link between you and someone else, you lay a stronger claim to the world.

And the beasts in the night have to go somewhere else to feed.

The Street of the Storytellers

The sun was almost gone, and dusk was moving into the Street of the Storytellers. In the golden evening light, passing through the long shadows, a young man approached the low wall where the old sages had always gathered. There were only a few here now, and the young man chose an empty spot, folding his legs under him, sitting. He unstrapped the pack of dog-eared papers he'd been carrying and put it down beside him.

The shadows of the huts and houses behind him were lengthening now, going far out across the empty street and into the breeze-blown field opposite, where dry stalks seemed to dance, dipping in and out of the sunlight, glinting now with minted gold, now lost in purple depths.

The young storyteller could feel the same chill wind rippling his clothing. He rubbed the dry skin of his face, and adjusted his position, feeling his bones creak.

In these moments before the arrival on this famous Street of those who would come to hear the stories, he thought about his new trade, and how he had come upon such a unique profession, among the more ordinary ways a man could earn his livelihood.

"A storyteller?" his father had boomed, disbelieving, when he had first told him of his decision. "Why not a juggler, or a balladeer, or a violin-player among the gypsies? Why don't you become a robber or a highwayman instead? It is just as shameful an occupation, and at least you would have some say in the money you kept! But a storyteller? You will have to plead for your pennies! You will be a beggar!"

And his mother, hearing, had cried, "My son, a beggar! Oh, pray he'll change his mind! My oldest son, my firstborn, doomed to beg on the street!"

And his father, turning: "See how you've made your mother weep."

"But remember all the tales I told to Yasmin and my little sister? Remember all the nights you scolded us for talking instead of sleeping? Remember the stories, father, that my brother and sister told you the next day, believing that they were real?"

"Yes, I remember. And I remember how angry I was that you, with your unruly imagination, should warp and twist the minds of your brother and sister. Because you told them fables, which is next to lying."

"But, father, remember how much pleasure it brought them? And how proud I was that they enjoyed my stories?"

"Yes, son. I remember."

"Well, father. I have learned that there are places, in the towns, where men gather on certain evenings, to do nothing but spin fables! These are called sages and storytellers, and others, men, women, and even children, come from the surrounding villages to sit in the evening and listen to these people, these sages, as they weave their fantasies. And if they like the tales, they pay them afterward!"

"But who would do such a thing? Who would drop all sensible, productive work to walk into a town and sit in a dusty street to listen to the babbling of a dreamer? Who?"

"I have heard that hundreds do such as you've described, father. I don't really know why. But, think for a moment. What made Yasmin and Shepila give up their sleep to pay attention to me, there in our beds? You know how much those two love to interrupt, and how easily their minds can wander. But something made them listen the whole time until my tale was done. Whatever made them sacrifice their sleep must also be what draws the listeners to the Street of the Storytellers."

His father paused. "But what is their payment?"

"Sometimes it is in coins, by those who have them. Or bread, cheese, wine or fruit by those who do not. It can also be clothes, a place to spend the night, a meal in someone's house, friendship. Whatever the payment, I have been told that the teller of a spellbinding tale can ask what he wants of his audience, and they will pay unquestioningly."

"Why would anyone do that?"

"Because they want to hear the rest of the story. It becomes a chain, binding the listener to the speaker. It makes slaves out of free men, by their own volition. The people who come to listen become addicted, and will do anything to hear more."

"I cannot believe that. It smacks of sorcery. Black magic."

"I have heard – "

"Perhaps those who told you all of these things were storytellers themselves!" His father laughed.

"Wouldn't such sorcerers be arrested?" said his mother. "Oh, my son, a player with magic most foul! To be condemned, and tortured – !"

"You would either be a beggar or a wizard," his father pronounced. "If you are one, you are below our family's status and we should despise you. If you are the other, it would be my duty to see that you died for your sins, for you might be possessed by demons. And in either case, I could not have my house under the stewardship of that kind of man. Your brother Yasmin shall be a tiller of the soil, a farmer. He will raise the crops, marry a wife and have a family of his own. He will not beg, nor practice witchcraft. Therefore, this will be his house...unless you reconsider."

"I won't change my mind. I know what I wish to do, what I would find the most enjoyment in doing. If that means I must relinquish my birthright, so be it."

And he had left his home.

He had packed up his clothes and belongings and had taken to the road.

Now, here he was, at a town he'd never known existed until he saw it at the end of a day's weary walking, sitting now in the shadows, waiting for the chance to practice his newfound skill.

What would be his story? What would be sure to draw to him the listeners he needed? Would an odyssey of danger and adventure be to their liking? Or a tale of terror and night spirits? Or a story of lovers and the power of their love? Or a narration of the exploits of soldiers in battle? Or adventurers on a quest? What story?

He searched through all the stories he remembered, ones he had told his brother and sister. Stories about gods and goddesses, about Pyromon, who ate tiger flesh and killed only those who murdered the innocent. Of Shedra and Moroc, who'd been kept apart by the battles of the City of Hate, unable to unite in eternal love because of the battalions of Moroc's family. He pondered these concepts, and many others.

The wind drowned the leaping wheat stalks in the field. This time they didn't spring back, all golden. The day was very old now, very old indeed. He could feel its chill in his legs. He had walked a long, long way this afternoon.

The newcomer looked to his right. Another storyteller had just arrived, and was sitting regally in his accustomed place, making himself comfortable. A large group of followers accompanied him. They brought him food, wine, and a carpet on which to sit. Others offered cushions for their idol, gifts of money and bread, fine clothes wrapped up, new-made robes and coats for him to wear. Listeners continued arriving, clustering around the revered one, none noticing the younger sage nearby. Nobody even looked his way. The young storyteller, sitting by himself, quietly envied his elder.

"Tell us the fate of Shalack the dark-haired marauder!" the crowd said.

"Did the blind man escape?"

"Where is Elicia hiding? Will she meet her lover before he must leave for the next battle?"

"Tell us about Brabhman!"

"What was behind the black door?"

"Where is the knife hidden?"

"Tell us!"

The honored gentleman raised a hand to acknowledge their questions. He took his time wrapping himself and taking a drink of the wine. The crowd leaned forward expectantly around him.

Whole families sat in the widening half-circle. People were taking out their own suppers to eat while they listened. Men filled their pipes and lit them. Their wives took out knitting to occupy their hands. Even the children were silent now. They nodded for the master to begin his tale. Young aspirants to the Storyteller's art also found places, and waited.

Now, the younger sage heard a shuffling of shoes on his left. He turned and saw a different storyteller taking his place. This one was younger than the first, and more handsome, with a pointed black beard.

He arranged his seating place, lighting lamps, setting out burners for incense, placing a leather satchel alongside him, which contained his papers.

He greeted the artists, intellectuals, and other devotees who arrived, grouping themselves around him, calling some of them by name. They returned the greetings, asking what story he would be adding another chapter to, tonight.

"I think I shall tell you of the noblewoman who had sixteen husbands, none of whom knew of the others. I trust you shall enjoy hearing of how she kept her multiple marriages a secret, and the effect her final revelation of the arrangements had on the more pompous ones among them."

The audience tittered in anticipation.

The shadows had grown together, becoming a pool of darkness under the open, empty sky.

The other storytellers were soon there, and had begun their tales of mirth and adventure, the young bearded one speaking in tones of gay irreverence, gesticulating magnificently, the older one droning on about his heroes and legends, while his listeners hung on each near-whispered word.

The youngest sage, new to this Street of the Storytellers, remained alone. He remembered something his father had said, the day he left home. 'How shall you earn your payment in a world of commerce and competition? If what you told me of this topsy-turvy profession of tale-telling holds truth, then you may be in for rugged times. Your brother and sister have listened because they had no other storytellers to distract them. You were without competition here.

'But if you go to this Street of the Storytellers, you will find yourself beset on every side by others older and wiser than you, who already have their followings and their fame assured. Even if someone sits to listen to you, the older sages will lure him away before your tale is finished, and you'll be left unpaid. I have known other tradesmen who have told me that this is true with them. Better masters will hound you out of business. And what then? You will have nothing!'

Was his father right? Was he a good storyteller only at home? Were his brother and sister the only audience he could ever depend on having?

The stars were coming out in the night sky. Down the street, somebody lit a lamp.

The audiences of the two other sages took up great areas, encroaching on each side, so that their perimeters nearly touched. Hardly any audience could be accommodated in the meager area left to the newcomer.

He could hear the tales of his neighbors, his colleagues, being spun on both sides. The words flowed over him in the otherwise silent evening air. He recognized the tales by their patterns. They were ones he had heard before, which had always held him fascinated. He listened raptly to them now, feeling the same enjoyment.

He wondered. Would he ever get the chance to tell a story like these others? His belly was empty, grinding on itself. His tongue was parched for wine, cool and red, from a donor's flask. His nostrils ached for the heady aroma of hot food. His back yearned for a tender bed in someone's house.

The thought of spending the coming night here, outdoors, gnawed at him.

The tale of Aklor and Iressa formed in his mind, of a poor man in love with a girl who possessed a magical wooden flying chair. Like his elder neighbor's tale, it would be a spinning-out of the efforts of two people to exist in a brutal, unsympathetic world, to escape the evils of war and prejudice, to find happiness in their love and achieve peace while surrounded by deceit and hypocrisy. Like that of the bearded intellectual, it would have humor, and wit, and contain many elegant puns and plays on words, and have moments of cynical irony plus rollicking satire.

He mulled it over, and considered how best to begin such a tale. He could tell it in the quiet manner of the elder sage, his voice lolling on a gentle tide of enchantment, words dripping from his tongue like nectar, to be caught only with effort so they could be tasted fully.

Or, he could tell it in the bold, clever manner of his colleague on the left, hands gesturing, forming images in the air, his eyes flashing, his voice rising and falling, the inflections calculated to hold attention, so that even half-asleep the listener would remain enthralled.

He could ask his listeners questions, so that they ended up taking part in the narrative. Or he could ignore them entirely, caring not if they heard or understood. He could be melodic and oratorical, or casual and informal. He could be like any of a dozen other storytellers people had told him about on his travels.

And this was probably wise, he thought. For, if their styles of telling, their choices of words, brought success, they would most assuredly do the same for him.

Wouldn't they?

Or would they, by being merely imitations, remind people of the original, sending them off to find what had inspired the mimic?

What if, to keep his listener, he employed the tricks he'd heard these others using?

False clues, for example, or 'had I but known' surprises. Or men in cupboards and snakes in baskets, women stripped of their clothes, cowering before the advancing rapist?

Technique, the manner of telling a tale, the mechanics of plot and grammar, left him pondering.

They got the young sage into such turmoil, there alone in the darkness, that he found himself measuring his tongue and his teeth, wondering whether he could speak at all.

The revelation came out of nowhere. It sat him up, and made him forget his worries. He saw the moon rising beyond the field, sliding upward like a vast circular lantern past the horizon.

What had an old master recently said?

"The moon does not know it is reflecting on the water, nor does the water know it is reflecting the moon. Yet the image remains, and is beautiful."

A bird doesn't know that anyone is listening to its song, and yet the song goes on.

It was the oldest and finest rule. When one tries the hardest, one does the least that is new and worthwhile. But when one stops struggling, suddenly it is all as he imagined it could be, if not better!

Being himself, he thought, he would have no competition!

There suddenly was the sound of shuffling before him. He looked forward. And there, right in front of him, he saw an unshaved, half-naked day laborer, his eyes blazing with anticipation, making himself comfortable.

"Tell me a tale," the man said. "I want to be entertained, to forget the hard work I had to do today. I wish to escape into a dream. Tell me a good story."

"I will. But first, I am hungry and cold, and tired from traveling."

"You may stay the night with me and my family. Our house is small, but we will make room for you." He glanced back and forth along the street. "I have listened to these others, and now I'm in a mood for something new. That's why I came to you as soon as I saw you." He looked even more steadily at the newcomer. "Now tell me the tale."

The young storyteller sat back. The smoke from his pipe curled into the air between him and his listener, scenting the dark.

"Have you been to the Vale of Karamar?" he said. "It is a place where perfumed lilies bloom in the lakes and blue-winged nightingales sing in the frankincense trees. And in its center, in a palace of carved jade, lives a princess named Iressa..."

Of A Yellow Summer

Howard Bell walked down his deserted street, surrounded by winter. Cold clouds filled the sky, impaled on the dark spires of ancient structures. A cutting wind razored its way through him, blowing swiftly uptown, hell-bent on freezing everything in its path. A scent of salt and old earth filled Bell's nostrils. He balanced on his aging feet and his long black cane, and peered into the rushing wind.

He was a veteran of many such winters, many more than he cared to remember. His face was craggy and scarred from their ravages, his skin was pale with their sunless dimness. His blue eyes were the color of ice, having faded from the summer-sky blue they had once been so long ago. His mind kept drifting back to those summers, days of wandering through yellow sun-glaring meadows and into black-shadowed oak groves, along winding trails leading through secret hollows, somewhere in countrysides long since forgotten.

As he walked, tipping his weight carefully from foot to cane to other foot, he slowly recognized an alien shape on the next street corner. It had been in his vision since he had left the entrance to the building where he lived, buttoning his long gray coat and adjusting his floppy-brimmed hat. Now he could see the stranger much more clearly. It was a dwarf, a dark little man half-hidden under a great enveloping jacket, a bright canvas cap perched on his nut-brown head. The dwarf stood in the midst of a fortification of cardboard cartons, on which were displayed dozens of identical, brightly-colored aerosol spray cans.

The dwarf called, in the voice of a creature that had been taken and pressed down and down in some great vise: "Summertime, summertime, summertime..."

Howard Bell gathered his bones tightly about himself and stood a moment, listening. The dwarf turned, sensing a presence, and looked at him with new-minted metallic eyes.

The wind blew.

"Step right up, mister, and have a look."

Howard took a step, and another step, and stood, looking down at the gnome-like apparition in the baseball cap. The dwarf's skin was the color of a Spanish saddle, and his eyes gleamed like Mexican silver. With a twitch and a lunge, he swung atop one of the boxes and faced Howard Bell squarely. "Summertime here," he said, holding up a can printed with baroque designs. "Ten cents, works like a miracle, available through this special offer for a short time only, and only from me."

He held out the can with a thrust.

Howard Bell took the can from the monkey-like hand of the dwarf, and turned it around. There was no discernible printing combined with the florid embellishments. It was metal, cool to the touch, like any ordinary spray can, and had a plastic top.

A wind blew, flavored with mint and spice.

"Summertime, you say?" said the old man.

"Summertime, yes sir," the dwarf replied. "Works like any spray deodorizer. Turns winter into summer, age into youth, sadness into pleasure. Just spray it in the privacy of your own home, and you will find that summertime comes to life before your eyes. Special offer, today only. Ten cents."

Howard Bell, taking his time, continued to inspect the can. The idea of summertime in a can fascinated him.

"Wanta buy?" said the dwarf.

"Ten cents?" the old man asked.

"Ten cents. Special offer."

Howard Bell finally dug into a great, gaping pocket of his coat, searching for the money he was to have spent on tobacco for his pipe. He wondered what scent the manufacturer might have put in the can and called summertime. What did summer smell like?

His gnarled white hand, at last, held out a dime.

Quickly the dwarf stuck out his hand and took the coin. After the exchange, Howard Bell slipped the can into the pocket where he had found the dime. Then, balancing on his cane, he turned and started home.

Behind him, in a wind which now smelled of burning wood, a squashed-in voice shrilled, "Summertime, summertime, summertime..."

It was a long way from the ground-level door, up the dark, narrow stairs toward the apartment where Howard Bell lived. He climbed patiently, placing cane and foot, cane and foot on the stairs, feeling the old wood creak in sympathy with his old bones, feeling the impenetrable depth of his weariness.

Finally he reached his door and opened it, stepping inside and then turning to shut it behind himself. Then he stepped forward and stood in the center of the room, his shoes planted on the faded patterns of his Oriental carpet, surveying a lifetime's gatherings of possessions as his eyes adjusted to the darkness. Then, slowly, he took the can from his pocket and set it on the small table next to his favorite reading chair. After he had attended to his many other discomforts, he would return, settle himself into the chair, and look at it. He went from room to room, in the meager light of drawn shades, returning finally to sit in the big, soft, overstuffed chair. He switched on his reading lamp.

He'd gotten his glasses, and now he put them on.

Working his fingers under an edge of the plastic cap, he pried it off. Holding the can out in front of him, he aimed the spray nozzle away from him in the silent air of the room, and then pressed the sprayer. A fine yellowish mist spread outward into the surrounding shadows.

It happened like a dream. The mist formed a circular opening in the air itself, from which bright summer sunlight shone, as though it was coming through an expanding iris. Like a lens, the ring of brilliance moved toward Howard Bell and encircled him, until the entire world was golden yellow.

He stared into the light, which flooded onto a grassy hill under a warm sky. Tree branches whispered overhead in a gentle afternoon breeze, and a path led away out of sight through the grass, between the dark trunks of gnarled oaks.

13

A surge of thrilled giddiness swept through Howard Bell, overwhelming him. He realized he was standing, had been on his feet all this time, and was nowhere near the aging easy chair where he had been sitting what seemed like only a few seconds ago. He rushed forward, slipped, staggered, and managed to regain his balance. He looked down at himself. He saw that he was a boy again, the age he had been the year when Amy died...

Howard Bell suddenly felt a swift, nameless urgency. Energy filled him, fiery and all-consuming. He wanted to run as fast as he could.

He took off through the summer-warm woodland, listening to the sounds around him, watching the path twist and turn among the trees. He raced to keep up with it, not tired, not out of breath, running at top speed as he thought about Amy.

He tripped and leaped and skidded down into a hollow filled with dried brown and yellow leaves, like parchment under his feet. The sun was warm above the tangled branches, but he wasn't perspiring. Instead of tweeds and woolens, he wore faded shorts and a striped cotton shirt. He stopped by a tree at the bottom of the woods, and listened. His mouth was dry from breathing, his feet tender from pounding the hot path. He caught his breath, feeling the warm air all around him and looking at the green leaves of the trees. Atop a nearby hill, yellow grass waved under a blue, utterly cloudless expanse of sky.

"Howie...!"

He listened. It was the voice of a young girl.

"Yoo-hoo!"

It was Amy's voice. Then he saw her, standing on the path in the distance, gazing back at him. She was summer-soft and summer-young, with eyes the color of the sky and hair as golden as the grassy, sunlit hillside rising behind her. The breeze rustled her short, lightweight cotton dress. She called again to him: "Howie!"

Howard Bell, whose whole long lifetime extended backward behind himself into infinity, couldn't remember the names of the hundreds of girls and women who had struck his momentary fancy during the years. But out of the farthest, most distant days of his past, Amy was still there in his memory, as bright and sweet as ever, his one, perhaps his only true love.

He ran toward her, but she laughed, turned, and started running too, up the grassy slope, heading for where its summit met the sky. He chased her, losing sight of her now and again, but always finding her around a turn of the path, closer and ever closer. He nearly had her in his reach, with her blonde hair flying, when everything dissolved into mist. Suddenly his feet were leaden, and his legs ached. He jerked, frightened, to a stop in his big overstuffed easy chair.

The aerosol can had fallen to the floor.

The rhythm of his running echoed in his brain. His eyes fought to find reality in the darkness of the room. Straining, he reached down and retrieved the metal can from the edge of the Oriental carpet. Had it been a dream?

He noticed his chair was cold. The jolt he'd felt upon awakening could have been his toppling backward into it. How long had he actually been sitting here?

And why, out of all the events he'd experienced in his life, had he dreamed about Amy? What day was it, that he had chased her out of the oak grove and up the yellow grassy hill, on a summer afternoon? Why had he felt such abrupt, unexpected urgency?

He rose and went to get himself something to eat, and as he fiddled with tin cans in the kitchen, he continued to probe into his memory.

The summer, the grass, the path and the oak grove haunted him. No dream had ever been so real before. It left him emotionally and physically drained, weary from surprise, excitement, and half-submerged terror.

And, as he turned out the last of the lights and climbed painfully into bed, he thought about the girl.

That summer, so long ago, had been a summer of many memories, when he was making most of the boyhood discoveries that revealed his world to him for the first time. It had been a summer of evenings by the river, afternoons in the woods, mornings in the aging Victorian house owned by his grandparents.

He remembered the special thing about that summer, about the particular day he'd just relived in the dream. It had a darkness which his mind didn't want to touch too closely.

That day held something dreadful and final.

He couldn't sleep as long as the images grew stronger in his mind.

He fought to extract every detail from what he could recall about that afternoon.

Yes, he knew, Amy had died that summer. But had it happened on that exact day, in that exact spot? And if so, how had it happened?

At two in the morning, with a fog of icy sorrows closing in on the windows of the bedroom, Howard Bell finally opened his eyes in the blackness as he felt the certainty sinking in.

Amy had indeed died that very afternoon.

The morning was as dismal and threatening as all the previous mornings had been, and Howard Bell awoke from a disturbed sleep to see steely clouds scudding low across the sky. Aching with cold, he tested his energies crossing the icy bedroom, dressed carefully, and went over to shut the window even tighter than before against the wind.

A long while later, after spending the morning reading a newspaper while drinking his breakfast coffee, he returned to his chair in the living room and sat, picking up the aerosol can.

He remembered that Amy had been killed suddenly in a gruesome accident on that summer day. He urgently wanted to return to her, to catch up with her on the path and hold her, to try somehow to save her. The thought crossed the back of his mind that, possibly, if he prevented her death in a dream from the summer aerosol, he could be with her now, in the present, in his old age, and his life would be different from the long bachelor existence it had in fact been.

This strange golden mist was his second chance at happiness, he told himself. It could give him another look at his love, and perhaps offer a way to rescue her from her fate, and mend his wasted life.

He pressed the sprayer.

As the past wrapped around him, he found himself standing again on his feet. He was young once more, the energy of youth surging through his body. The breeze from the clear blue sky caressed him. He sprang forward on the dusty path.

And Amy was there as she had been before, running very close to him, heading up the yellow hill in the sunshine, and he had his boyish hand out to grab at her streaming yellow hair. He got a hold of it, and they tumbled together around a bend in the path. They fell, laughing, into a bed of soft, dry weeds.

He felt the solid warmth of Amy's body in his grasp, the touch of her hands, and saw the playful glimmer in her blue eyes.

While he lay on his back a moment later, breathing the warm summer air, which was laden with scents of ripe grass, she sat up and surveyed the smoothly rounded contours of the hills encircling them both.

In the distance, a dark building huddled among a cluster of dense green oaks, at a point where a small stream babbled over rocks, cascading from a shelf of mossy boulders into a clear pool.

He sat up beside her.

"What's that?" she said, pointing at the building.

"The old grist mill," he replied.

"It looks spooky."

"Been abandoned a long time."

The old Howard Bell, living in the brain of the boy, almost as though he was in a city bus looking out through the windows of the boy's eyes at the passing scene, watched his younger self walk down a side trail toward the dilapidated mill by the stream, with Amy moving ahead of him.

He wanted to scream for her to stay away from the mill, but the two personalities sharing the interior of Howie's head fought a silent war with each other, the man ordering the boy to do something, the boy struggling in turn for the right to explore this fascinatingly sinister place.

The stream near the mill was bridged by an old log which had fallen from one bank to the other. The path led to the log, and over it to the opposite side.

"Let's go in the mill," Amy said.

"Why?" the older Howard asked, speaking with the mouth of the boy.

In his brain, he remembered hearing and seeing all of this before, a long lifetime ago.

"Because I want to," she said. "Come on!" She ran down the path to the fallen log, then stepped quickly across it to the other side. Howard had to follow her, and he raced to catch up.

He saw her disappear inside. Entering after her, he found her prowling among the dark wooden supports. The interior of the old mill was cold and deep, like a cave, with massive timbers leaning inward on all sides. The wood smelled of age, mold and neglect.

"Hey, it's cold in here," he heard himself say.

Amy wandered between the aging timbers. "Isn't it wonderful?" she said, grinning back at him through the enclosed, dust-laden air.

All at once the place looked very threatening to the older Howard Bell. He knew that there wasn't much time left for him to take control of Howie the boy. He strained, also, to recall what it was that would be happening next.

"Let's explore, Howie," Amy suggested.

"Amy, we'd better get out of here," he gasped.

"What?" she said, staring at him.

"You're going to get hurt," he said, his voice filled with terror.

"What's wrong with you?" she blurted.

"I...I don't like the looks of this place."

She frowned. "But – " she started to say.

He rushed toward her, reaching for her. But she retreated. "Howie, it's nice in here. Come on, Howie!"

There was an edge of fright in her tone.

He shook his head. "No, no, Amy! Let's go."

She turned away from him. "Well," she said, "if you want to be a fraidy-cat, you can leave. I'm going to look around. It's fun, being in here – "

Something huge creaked and groaned over their heads. A board snapped and flopped down, rattling.

Amy froze. "What was that?"

Howard grabbed at her once again. A tremendous cracking noise sounded. Amy went pale, her eyes suddenly bulging in fear.

In front of them, blocking their only path of escape, a huge timber began to crack, splintering.

"Howie – !" Amy moaned.

Howard Bell, the old man, instantly remembered. He had fled the last time for his own safety! He had abandoned Amy in the mill as it fell apart. She had died, while he had survived to grow old alone.

Quickly now, he dragged the screaming girl by her arm, pulling her forward in spite of her panic, under the sagging beam. Its vast dark bulk descended slowly, separating. With all his strength, ignoring her yelps of pain, he flung her ahead so that she dropped into the dust and rolled over, shouting angrily, turning to look back at him with the beginnings of an accusation on her lips.

At that moment, however, gigantic unseen weights started tearing loose above.

Amy made a weak sound in her throat.

"Quick, Amy, get out!" Howard yelled.

She retreated, horrified, toward the sunlit entrance. The old mill had chosen this moment to die.

The ceiling caved in over Amy's head. She covered her eyes with her hands, screaming.

The millstone! Howard's mind howled.

He remembered now. Long after dark, the rescuers had found Amy in the wreckage, under the massive gray granite stone, crushed to death. Frigid with the realization that he had about half a second left to live, Howard shouted one last time for Amy to get clear. She turned and fled obediently, dropping forward, face down, as the doorframe collapsed.

Looking up, Howard saw the giant stone booming down toward him through the shattering ceiling. He felt its entire weight settle onto him as he reached out toward Amy, who lay in the dirt below the outside steps, weeping.

She had made it, this time.

It was too late for him.

The old woman walked down a deserted city street, surrounded by winter. She was alone, as she had been these last seventy years. Though she had searched all her life, she had never found a boy she loved as much as her girlhood companion, Howard Bell.

She could still clearly recall the warm midsummer afternoon, so long ago, when the mill where she had led Howard, wanting to explore its depths, had suddenly and incredibly started to collapse onto them both. She remembered how Howard had sacrificed himself to make sure that, no matter how she objected to the way he manhandled her, she would wind up clear of the falling granite millstone. She could still see the giant stone dropping onto the dirt floor of the mill, crushing him as she watched.

She had undergone therapy for years, and the psychiatrists had finally been able to dispel most of her nightmares about the abandoned mill out of her mind.

Ahead now, far down the street, an alien shape caught Amy's eye. It was a dwarf, a creature unbelievably compressed and wrinkled, wearing a floppy coat and a canvas baseball cap, standing atop a fortification of cardboard cartons on which were displayed dozens of identical, brightly colorful aerosol spray cans, printed with Baroque designs.

The dwarf held one of the cans aloft, in a nut-brown hand.

And, in a voice as ancient and squeezed-in as his body, the dwarf, something unnatural and foreign to an ordinary world, called out repeatedly, "Summertime, summertime, summertime...!"

A wind was blowing, a wind flavored with mint and spice, possessing the timeless scent of burning wood.

The Hole

From the minute John found the hole, he knew what it could do to him. He pushed aside the folded-over carpeting and the heavy sheet of discolored plywood that had covered it, getting down on his hands and knees. He crept closer to the edge of the hole, and looked into it.

A gust of dank, chilly air blew up out of the hole against his face. John gasped in sudden terror. It was a smell of wet, lifeless, rotting things.

He jerked convulsively back from the odor.

Afterward, waves of panic ebbed gradually away in him, like ripples on a cold pool. He felt that he was being literally pulled into the hole, as though he was helpless to prevent himself from falling in. The darkness beneath the floor seemed to want to reach up and out like a huge black hand, to grab him and drag him down. Here was a portal leading into an infinity of nothingness, yawning only a few feet away. John was a man who had just come face-to-face once again with the single great dread of his life.

And it sickened him. His stomach rebelled, and, retching, he climbed unsteadily to his feet and turned, lurching into the nearby bathroom to be fully sick in the toilet bowl.

Just then, Mary strode in from the patio, crossing the distant living room. She called to him cheerily, walking through the house. "John, could you help me for a moment outside?"

This was their first weekend in the new place, a rambling one-story

Spanish-style hacienda surrounded by an acre and a half of tiled walkways, dark ancient overhanging oaks, and overgrown landscaping. Mary had been spending the day putting up trellises and checking the condition of the rose garden, while John had come upon the unexpected unevenness in the thick hall carpeting, now made prominent by the clear light of midday. He had taken the carpet up, removed the plywood, and discovered the hole.

She stepped into the hallway. "John?"

"Look out!" he croaked from the bathroom. "There's a bottomless pit in front of you, in the floor!"

She glanced down, having almost put one foot into the hole before she realized what it actually was. "Oh, my!" she blurted. A chip of the original hardwood flooring that she had kicked with her shoe dropped over the rim and sailed silently down into the blackness.

"What's this hole doing here?" she asked calmly.

His face ashen, John hurried out into the hall and clutched her. "Thank God you're all right!"

She shrugged free. "Of course I am. But why the devil is there a hole like this in our hallway?"

She extended one foot out over the lightless maw.

"Crazy damn place for a hole to be, isn't it."

He wasn't able to watch.

"It was under the...the carpeting."

"Well well well," she said with a slightly derisive snort. "That real-estate agent certainly kept this a secret, didn't he."

"It was covered with an old piece of plywood."

"I see, I see..." She continued prodding the rotting plank. "Do you think it can be repaired? The floor, I mean."

"I don't know – " He shook his head, took one more look into the pit, then left the hallway, pushing past Mary and heading down the paneled entryway beyond, into the kitchen. She gave the hole another concerned glance, then followed her husband.

She found him sitting at the white-painted service table, lighting a cigarette, his hands shaking. This concerned her, because John had promised not to fill this clean new house with cigarette smoke the way he had done in their apartment, and as a result he'd been trying to quit all week. He hadn't lit one of his Winstons in at least three days.

Sitting down across from him, she set her forearms on the tabletop. "Well?" she insisted. "Can you fix the floor?"

He took a long pull on the cigarette, and blew out a cloud of smoke. "John," she said. "What's wrong with you? Does the sight of a silly hole disturb you this much?"

His reply, when it came, was only half-audible. "I couldn't even look into that hole without getting sick to my stomach," he mumbled. "It's my one real phobia. I've always been afraid of bottomless empty spaces, caves, mineshafts, wells. I had a bad run-in with one when I was a kid. I was probably about five or six, when my younger brother and I found one in a field on my uncle's farm. Neither of us expected the ground around it, hidden under wet weeds, to be as slippery as it was. When I tried to get closer, to see down inside it, my leg slipped and I slid all the way in. I ended up only hanging on by my hands while Brian ran for help. Christ, I didn't think he was ever gonna come back..."

"But they pulled you out, finally, didn't they?" Mary reminded him.

"Sure. My uncle brought a rope, threw it to me, and everybody thought it was a big joke after they hauled me out and we went back to the house. But I have nightmares about it even now. I'm scared to death of holes, especially of falling into one. If you tossed a rock into that hole in the hallway, and I watched it go all the way down, I think I'd curl up and die, right then and there."

He held out both his hands, the Winston still smoldering between the fingers of his left.

"See? Already I can't hold 'em still."

She looked, and shook her head.

"John! Phobia, schmobia. Really!"

"What're you saying?" he asked, peering desperately across the table at her.

"I'm saying that I don't believe it. You're a grown man! Maybe little kids are afraid of the boogeyman or the dark, but you...?" She probed him with her gimlet eyes. She was an intelligent, forceful woman, prone to rock-solid definitions of the way things were, and the firm taking of stands for or against whatever she felt was important.

"You, darling," she said, "a man who spent two years in the service, worked in Alaska and on the Gulf Coast when you were getting your start, got into fights, got shot at, even...How can you suffer from such an inane thing as a fear of holes in the floor? I mean, are you kidding or something?"

"No," he replied sadly.

"Well then," she said with even greater firmness in her voice. "What you need is some good logical reassurance. Everybody has their problems, I guess. But all you have to remember is this. It's just a hole."

His next look at her was wild and panicky:

"It scares the hell out of me, Mary!"

She harrumphed. "A few facts. It won't bite you. If you're careful, you don't even have to think about it. After all, it's only a few feet wide. Certainly less than six feet deep underneath the house. It was probably dug by hand in the last century. There used to be a lot of old Spanish ranches around here. And this particular house was obviously built right over one of the wells, which hadn't been properly filled-in."

"But," John said, lighting his third cigarette since they'd sat down, "why did they have it covered with nothing but a piece of plywood, right there under the carpeting, in the hallway, where people have to walk?" His whole frame gave a shudder.

"I'd say that after the well originally caved in again, the floorboards rotted away. This isn't a new house, you know. The agent says it's been here since the Twenties, which incidentally is why it's so fantastically charming! And if there's some unexpected fixing-up that has to be done, that probably explains why we were able to get this mansion for such a song!"

John shook, sucking in his breath unsteadily. "See what I'm saying?" he exhaled. "There's something horrible and rotten down there at the bottom of that hole. That is, if it has a bottom at all. A body? The corpse, or corpses, of all its earlier victims? Damn it, Mary, something rotted out those floorboards, and was starting to do a pretty good number on the sheet of plywood as well. Some repair job the last owners of this deathtrap did, that's all I've got to say..." His voice trailed off as he concentrated on lighting his next cigarette in his old way, off the still-fuming butt of the previous one.

Mary's look of distaste was rapidly souring into outright anger. "Stop it!" she spat. "You're behaving like a four-year-old!"

"I don't care!" he said defiantly. "There it is. And no floor, no supports, no nothing to keep us safe. Just a damn pit right in the middle of our new house, waiting to suck us both down to our deaths! I'm halfway toward believing that something really sinister has been going on in this place since it was built, something deadly and ghastly, maybe involving cannibalism, or demon worship, or just a cult of ritual murder! How else can you explain a hole that was not too cleverly concealed where we would be walking to get to the bathroom, to the goddamned bathroom for Christ's sake, which nobody bothered to warn us about? Not even the real-estate agent!"

As Mary stared at him, he kept his eyes fixed for the moment on the tabletop.

"We should never have taken this house, at any price," he muttered bleakly. "We're going to have to give it up. As sunny and romantic and charming as you might think it is, darling, it's a deathtrap, and we're its next intended victims..."

"The hell we are," she finally said, standing up. "I'm not giving up this place. That is nothing but a simple hole in the ground, just waiting for somebody clever enough, and grown-up enough, to get busy and repair it!"

When he continued to refuse to look at her, she came around the table and pulled the cigarette out of his hand, mashing it into the ashtray, which had been sparkling-clean until just a few minutes ago. Then she took his hand and pulled him to his feet.

"Come on, baby," she said flatly.

"Where are you taking me?"

"I'm gonna help you snap out of this fit you seem to be having. You're gonna see just how silly it's been for you to get this worked-up. It's time you saw that the hole is just a hole, and nothing in the world to be so afraid of."

"I can't do it, Mary. Don't make me."

"You're an idiot." She dragged him by the hand, out of the kitchen, across the entryway, into the inner hallway where the bedrooms were. He went along blindly, but started to pull back as they came closer to the hole. "Here, I'll hold your hand for you," she said mockingly. "You don't even have to look into the hole if you don't want to."

"Let me go..."

"Not a chance, John."

Her tone was enough of a challenge for him to open his eyes and take a look. As he did, his dizziness, plus the accompanying nausea, returned full-force.

"Yoo-hoo," Mary called playfully into the pit.

It was an obscene black mouth, a travesty in what was supposed to be one of the safest parts of the house. Its edges were lined with rot-tipped floorboards, like teeth. Its breath was chill and foul. Its interior left everything to John's imagination. Any or all nightmares could be conjured, any monsters composed of slime and eyes could be created in the subconscious, to populate its depths.

Echoes of Mary's hoot rang all the way down the circular walls.

He didn't even notice that she'd left him alone, until she returned with a flashlight that she'd gotten from a kitchen drawer. Clicking it on, she aimed the beam downward into the hole and pointed it this way and that. Smooth adobe brickwork reflected the dim light dully. The center remained featureless and black.

Alongside her, John stared abjectly downward, trembling, swallowing.

"See how easily you can look, once you understand it?" she said with total pragmatism. "It's a perfectly simple, ordinary – "

But she didn't go on. John had whirled away from her, stumbling into one of the bedrooms and slamming the door.

Mary shrugged, switched off the flashlight, lifted the plywood sheet over the hole, then set the carpeting back down over that.

For two weeks she found it impossible to get John to look at the hole again. He spent the next day shopping for a new piece of plywood, twice as large and half again as thick as the old one, which he proceeded to give several coats of preservative oil, before he ordered Mary to put it in place over the hole, while he hid in the kitchen.

Every time after that, whenever she expressed interest in repairing the hole, John quietly found something else to do.

At last, out of desperation, she phoned her brother Sam and his wife Marie, who lived only a few miles away, and asked them to drop by whenever it was convenient, so that Sam might look at the hole and decide what could be done about it. At the promise of dinner and drinks, Sam, who was in the construction business, readily agreed to come.

Mary showed him the hole, and he frowned.

"How deep do you think it is?" she asked him.

"Have you shone a flashlight into it?"

She nodded. "But you still can't see the bottom."

John was elsewhere, with Marie, avoiding Mary and Sam, and the hole in the hallway.

"Must be pretty deep, then," Sam concluded. "You're probably facing some major work, if you want this thing filled-in. It could be expensive."

"How about us doing it ourselves?" she asked. "Could it be done?"

With his hand on his chin, Sam stepped around the hole, looking into it from various directions. At last he nodded. "Maybe. We could set in a framework of two-by-fours, about a dozen feet down, then follow that with wire mesh and tarpaper, plus more wire for reinforcing. Then if we could get the chute from a cement mixer through one of the bedroom windows, we could pour in a concrete plug. The whole thing ought to last for years. Finally we'd wheel in several loads of dirt, after which it'd be no problem replacing the joists and the flooring."

Mary smiled. "That sounds fine. Do you want to help us do it?"

Sam put his arm around her. "Be glad to, sis."

"But," she said a few minutes later, when everyone was back once again in the living room, "you're not going to have to do it all by yourself. I swear I'll have that fraidy-cat husband of mine give you a hand, if it's the last thing I do!"

She hurried off to find John, who turned out to be puttering among his books in the teak-lined study at the end of the far wing, opposite from the bedrooms, as remote from the hole as he could get and still be inside the house.

She towed him the entire way to the bedroom wing, by force.

"No," he kept saying weakly, "don't make me do it – !"

Sam and Marie followed the two of them into the hallway, giving each other wondering glances.

"You're going to get used to that hole, and that's all there is to it!" She gripped his arm. "Here we are. Now look at it!"

He covered his eyes.

She wrestled with him, pulled his hands away. "Look!" she shouted into his face. "Look, will you? I didn't marry a worm, I married a man! It's just a goddamn hole!"

"Yes, it's only a hole," repeated Sam behind them, as though he felt he had to say something. "Honest, John. It's perfectly safe."

Staring down, John began to whimper. Tears sprang from his eyes.

"A grown man," Mary said to her brother and sister-in-law, "Afraid of a stupid *hole* in the floor!"

But John was changing. Bit by bit. His breathing had grown shallow. His complexion was becoming increasingly waxy. His eyes were dilated like the yolks of raw eggs. Every sinew in his body had hardened into a cord. He could feel the darkness rising out of the pit to reach him. He shrank away from it, despite the people surrounding him. He felt that he was trapped, doomed, a waiting sacrificial victim.

The evil which lived in the hole was free once again, and it had already noticed him.

And it was coming to take him...

"See, darling?" said Mary, standing beside him. "Nothing has happened. It's just an old well, and when we're through fixing it no one'll even know it's there. Now, don't you feel silly?"

The Thing made a grab for him. John flailed mindlessly back, blubbering, thrashing, fighting to save his life. The Monster was there, huge and real, clawing at him. He beat against Sam and Mary in order to escape from doom, whirling away from it. The talons of the nightmare vision, towering now at his back, touched his shoulders.

In his headlong flight he didn't notice his wife losing her balance and dropping into the pit.

Her fading shriek went on for a long, long time.

"Oh, my God...!" said Sam.

Later, while Marie called the police, Sam stayed where he'd been since it had happened, gaping, staring down into the suddenly-very-frightening hole.

Trudy's Eyes

This is what happened.

The fights began when Trudy and I were kids. Mom and Dad spent hours shouting, throwing things, and slamming doors. I went outside with Trudy whenever this was going on. We hid out back, and pretended we were alone and nobody could bother us.

Even then there was something strange about Trudy's eyes.

What do I mean? You know when you see a light at night very far away? And how you begin feeling that you're falling toward it, that it's pulling you closer and closer? That was how it was with her eyes.

She always looked straight at me whenever we were alone together, looked at me without blinking, with those huge, dark eyes. I couldn't keep looking back at them for very long, without feeling as if I was being somehow sucked out of myself. Trudy and I had more secrets between us, and knew more private ways of signaling to each other, than I suppose you could say was normal between a brother and sister.

Maybe it's because we were twins, being born only about four or five minutes apart. But whatever the reason, all we had to do was look at one another, no matter where we were, to know what we were both thinking.

Later on, the thing we shared between us grew stronger. If Trudy knew that Dad was on the way home, and Mom was laying in wait for him, she would find me, and the two of us would go out back.

The fights between Mom and Dad continued until Trudy and I were in junior high school. By then they'd gotten worse. Dad would beat

Mom, and Mom would throw things at him, not just to scare him but to really try and hurt him. It got pretty bad.

Then suddenly it was over.

Mom called the police one night when Dad was in a killing mood. The two of them spent a morning in court. Dad moved out, Mom stayed in the old house, and I stayed with her, and got a job, and spent most of my time hanging out somewhere else.

The only bad thing was that Dad, with the approval of the judge, had taken Trudy.

Although I wandered around a lot at night, I never met any girls with eyes like Trudy's. I wanted to feel the impact of those eyes again, badly.

So one evening when I'd found out where Dad lived (he was always moving from one apartment to another), I sneaked over to see Trudy. I waited on the street outside the building until I saw Dad go out. Then I went upstairs. The place was old, and cheap, with smelly, dismal, badly-lit corridors. It broke my heart to think that this was where my twin sister was living. Finally I found the right door, and knocked, and waited. Eventually Trudy unlocked it and opened it. She looked more intensely at me as soon as she realized who I was. Then, even though she was alone, she let me in.

We talked.

That was all we did that first night. Just talked. I asked her personal questions, secret questions. And she answered every one, as though she'd known all along what I was going to be asking.

I asked her about Dad.

Suddenly, Trudy was crying.

Dad had gone after her, she said, had grabbed her, had pushed himself onto her...and into her. It was something you'd have to be a girl to understand, she said, raising her eyes and focusing them directly on mine...to understand how terrible it made you feel on the inside – how helpless.

She'd fought him off as much as she could.

But he was so much bigger...

As she told me about this, speaking in a breathless, deep, penetrating voice, I suddenly realized that I did understand.

I began feeling like I'd been raped myself.

Trudy told me about how Dad had promised that when he got back later tonight he would continue teaching her how to show him the proper respect, the way he said he deserved on account of the fact that he was her father. His method for teaching her consisted of slapping her around, pulling her hair, calling her a whore and a slut, then dragging her into the bedroom.

It finally dawned on me how intensely she'd begun staring at me, the whole time we'd been talking. Somewhere deep inside the vast darkness of her eyes was the light, piercing the air of the dingy, brown-walled, poorly lighted room. It was as though something about her eyes was drilling right into me, penetrating my skull. It was like I was being lifted out of the chair and pulled forward across the room, to fall through Trudy's eyes and into another universe. It was the way you'd fall down a well in a nightmare, unable to grab the sides, screaming without making a sound, all the way to the bottom.

If there's a difference between males and females, it's the way each one thinks. The males are always extending themselves outward to learn what lies beyond the next barrier. And the females keep pulling everything in, swallowing it up, sucking it into the depths of dreams, searching for desire, or revenge, with an intensity that males have never known.

Trudy surrounded me. We mingled. Reality spun around me. I was stretched and pulled and torn loose from myself. I was squeezed through a gap and into another skin, poured back and forth in space.

Then I was free. I pulled back from my sister's eyes.

And it was like I was looking into a mirror, only it wasn't a mirror.

I was looking at myself.

I had somehow ended up *inside* Trudy, while she had entered me. A secret thrill flashed through me. It was embarrassing. It was also incredibly erotic. I was sitting on the other side of the room, and everything was reversed.

I wasn't looking at Trudy. I was looking at myself. Can you understand what I'm saying? I had on my clothes. And I smiled.

But I was not me! I was her! I was wearing her skirt, and I could feel the weight of her hair resting on my shoulders. I was small, shapely, petite. My hands were like doll's hands. My fingers were long and slender. Her shoes were on my feet, which were small enough to fit comfortably in them.

I felt a nasty tingle deep within me as I thought about the girl's secret parts hidden under this skirt, between my thighs. I was the hollow one now, not Trudy.

But I was Trudy! If I moved my arms or my legs, I feared I could go crazy. I sat gripping my knees with her hands.

The effect lasted for only a few seconds. Then I fell back through the invisible membrane again.

I can't recall anything else about that night. All I knew was that, after I went home, I wanted to go on seeing Trudy again and again afterward. It became a regular thing.

What did we do?

For one thing, it didn't involve sex. After all Dad had done to her, Trudy couldn't stand letting any man touch her. But that didn't mean she wasn't fascinated with the mysteries that made boys different from girls, males from females. So instead of touching and groping, Trudy and I did other things.

She sat across from me and talked about the feelings going on inside her body, the warm things she often noticed happening when a certain emotion gripped her, the receptiveness she felt. Girls, she said, are minus something, the same way that boys are plus. Girls have a lack, a gap that needs to be filled, while boys have too much, something extra. Boys' minds, she said, had as many things sticking out as their bodies. Boys pushed. The male spirit jutted out, she believed, seeking and probing, poking and prodding, invading everything it didn't understand in its search for the inner truth. Dad was like this, and because he was a man he really couldn't help it.

She asked me if this wasn't true, and I admitted that it probably was, though I'd never heard it put exactly that way before. I knew I'd done this myself, all my life, exploring every gap and hollow, every dark place, every opening. And I'd always wondered why girls didn't feel the same way.

Girls weren't probers, Trudy said. Instead, they waited. They were like empty vessels, needing to be filled. A girl who wasn't loved, she said, felt hollow and useless. She wanted me to supply her with dreams, entering her brain and moving through her body, pushing myself into all her most secret places.

So I told her my dreams. I described my fantasies, the private visions I had always had about girls. I had never told anyone else about these daydreams. But Trudy was special. I gave Trudy images to think about that she would've never discovered on her own. She'd never been interested in learning these things by herself, she said. She needed to have a man who would plant such ideas in her imagination for her.

"You're making me pregnant with ideas," she said one afternoon, beaming unexpectedly at me. "Before you began coming to visit, I always felt so empty. Now I feel full."

Along with thoughts and ideas, Trudy and I also started showing each other the private parts of our bodies. It was as if we were giving each other a precious, personal gift.

It was a hot night the next time I visited Trudy. She was shaking as she opened the door. I grabbed her and held her, wondering if she was having a nervous breakdown. She hadn't been in such bad shape since the time she'd sucked me out of my body with her eyes.

Dad, she said, had raped her again that afternoon.

I came inside and slammed the door. I was mad. I paced back and forth across the room trying to figure out how I could get revenge for what Dad had done. The window was open, and I went over and stood for a while staring down into the street, at the parked cars, the lights, and the passing pedestrians. Behind me, Trudy asked me to please come back and sit down. But I didn't move. I couldn't stop shaking with fury. Finally she rose and moved toward the window, coming up behind me. Suddenly her arms slipped around me and she nuzzled the side of my neck with her lips.

Turning me around, she led me toward the sofa again, where we sat down side by side, her body pressing warmly against me. She told me what Dad had done. She spoke slowly, and answered my questions in detail. We became more intimate than ever as she described the rape.

Gradually, she talked me out of getting even with Dad. The old bastard was sick, she said. He would never get another chance to do what he had done. She had already made up her mind about that. I didn't know what she meant.

In a moment she got to her feet. She paused to smooth her skirt with her hands, standing in front of me, so close that I became aware of the smell of her body. Her long brown hair draped down behind her like a veil.

She was my twin sister. But the desire I suddenly felt had nothing to do with filial affection. It was a longing, a wishing, a yearning, a desolate wanting.

Slowly, Trudy moved away. Her hips shifted with a uniquely female swivel. I could taste the allure of her, and sense it oozing from her, especially for me. She turned and sat in the other chair, facing me.

Her eyes were dark and gigantic. As soon as I saw the light appearing deep inside them, I couldn't look away.

They blazed.

The room began to sparkle with whirling stars. The dirty walls disappeared. I had no feeling anymore. I floated in a silvery universe, in a sky with no top, no bottom.

A stupendous force pulled me forward. I lost my balance, and fell into the starry tunnel.

It was a long, long way down into the world of Trudy's eyes.

After a moment, I recovered. I was sitting normally again, in the grubby room of Dad's apartment, in the dim glow of the single lamp.

I focused on my sister.

A shuddering chill gripped me as I thought about the terrible thing that had just happened. My masculinity was gone. The throbbing power that my earlier anger had given me was no longer there.

There was nothing but a warm space between my legs, where a dull ache still throbbed – the physical memory of what had happened when Dad had tried teaching my sister a lesson by raping her.

The boy who had been me, who still was me on the outside, stood up and walked toward the front door of the apartment. He kept smiling as he glanced back over his shoulder at me. I was too numb to do anything. He got his jacket and put it on. I remembered what it had always felt like to put my arms into the sleeves of that jacket. But now it was somebody else, not me!

"So long...Jake," he said, speaking in my voice. It sounded different now that I was hearing it from outside my own head. But I still recognized it.

In a few seconds the door closed and I was alone in the room. I didn't dare move. I didn't know what would happen to this female body if I tried to.

Then, through the open window, I heard Dad hollering outside, down in the street. "Jake!" he bellowed, his voice echoing off the other buildings, up and down the block. "Were you upstairs, talkin' with Trudy? Puttin' more rebellious ideas into her head? I warned her what I'd do if you came around here again! Jake? Come back here, you son of a bitch! Jake! Don't you run away from me! *Jake!* JAKE!!"

I heard their feet pounding away into the distance as Dad chased furiously down the street after Jake. I had often fled from Dad when he was crazy mean. I could see myself trying to escape from him now, once again.

But it wasn't me running. It was him. I still sat here in this room, frozen, unable to move. I wanted Jake to come back, wanted me to reappear so I could get into my own body again, and not be what I had become.

Someone screamed a long way off, down the street. It wasn't a human shriek.

It was the squeal of tires on pavement.

I heard Dad shout.

I don't think I can go on with this.

It's too much. I can't do it – !

No...no, I'm all right. Honest, I'll be okay. I'll be fine. Only – oh, God! God!

Okay...okay, okay. I'm okay now.

Anyway, Dad came back. His shoes thumped up the apartment stairs. He opened the door. He was carrying my jacket, his son's jacket. It was torn almost in half, and there was a lot of blood.

A distant siren wailed outside.

He told me what had happened. Jake was dead.

He grinned with obvious pleasure when he said it. He gave me a look that was sheer meanness.

"You're all mine now," he said. "Jake's not here any longer to take you away from me."

I couldn't get moving. I wanted to move, as Dad threw down the bloody jacket and came toward me with his hands lifting forward and moving apart to grab me out of the chair. But it was like trying to swim up from deep underwater, like digging my way free from the bottom of a filled-in grave.

I gasped for air. I think I screamed, though it wasn't my voice I heard, but Trudy's. I was more aware than ever of my smallness, my vulnerability. It sickened me.

It was this eruption of panic that finally brought me to my feet. I jumped up, out of Dad's reach, and was astonished at the lightness of my body. A girl's body. My sister's body.

I remembered the kitchen knife.

It was one of Trudy's memories, not mine. But now that I had her brain, inside her skull, I knew everything she'd learned. She knew where the knife would be, in one of the drawers on the right-hand side of the sink. It was the only thing our combined minds could think of for me to use, to defend myself. I headed into the kitchen as Dad lumbered after me, knocking over furniture, crashing into doorframes, roaring with fury.

The drawers swam into view. I clawed the top one open with my frighteningly thin, insubstantial hands. It contained spoons and forks, but no knives.

Dad caught me as I opened the second drawer, my fingers fumbling inside. He gripped me with hands that felt as powerful as steel clamps. Something in the drawer sliced my flesh, the warm blood flowing. I took hold of a wooden handle and whipped whatever it was out into the open.

Dad swung me around with shocking force. If I had been me, I would've thrown all my 180 pounds into battling him, which might've been enough, if I was lucky.

But Trudy's 100-pound body was too slender to have any effect against such overwhelming strength. Was this the way my sister had always felt, at the mercy of my father's rage?

Dad's acid breath washed over me in a nauseating cloud as he leaned down to fasten his mouth onto mine.

The hand with the knife moved by itself, guided somehow by a remnant of my sister's consciousness that still lived in the muscles, bone, and sinews of my pale tapering arm.

The blade slid into meat, crunched against gristle, twisted past bone. Dad gasped, jerking his mouth away. This was what Trudy had sworn she would do, the next time Dad attacked her, and now she had done it. His eyes went feral, wild, rolling in their sockets. But the knife went on stabbing. Twice. Three times. Four. It didn't want to stop.

Dad's fists were around my throat as he began to weaken. All his weight was pressing against me, there in the kitchen. I let go of the knife and heard it clatter onto the floor. A streak of blood had been flung back on the opposite wall, the droplets glistening as red as barn paint on the soiled yellow enamel.

With the last of my fading energy I pushed Dad off me and stumbled out through the living room toward the door, heading for the sounds of those sirens.

And so here I am. The rest you know.

And I'm really Trudy's brother Jake. I'm a man, trapped in a girl's body! It was never what I really wanted. She did it without my desiring it, stealing my body away from me, and leaving me with something else, a thing that has an emptiness in it, instead of a surplus, and it's not fair!

I want my body back!

I want *me* back!

Strange Lover

When she first thought she saw it, on a quiet sunlit afternoon, the tingle that flashed down the middle of her bare, exposed back told her that it was alive, and that it was watching her.

Annabelle, blonde, attractive, and in her twenties, worked as private secretary for an important executive whose office was located in one of the nearby glass-and-steel high-rise towers.

But this was a slow season of the year, and so her boss hadn't bothered asking her to come in and work overtime on Saturday.

It was mid-July, and the temperature was blistering hot, even here on the western edge of the city, with the cool ocean lying only a few miles away. Late this morning, when the temperature outside had already passed ninety degrees, she had decided that her best defense against the heat was to spend the long, lazy day in her apartment bedroom with the shades drawn, her electric fan softly whirring in a corner, while she lay nude on her unmade double bed and read from her vast collection of paperback romances.

Annabelle loved such stories, even though she was perfectly aware of how stupid they were, and how little they related to the ordinary, mundane problems of working girls in everyday life.

What she liked most about them were the heroes, tender, sensitive, gentle fellows, each one not only unbelievably good-looking but disgustingly wealthy, with oodles of free time on their hands, no matter that they all seemed to be holding down responsible, important positions as captains of commerce and industry. Their bronzed chests, their chiseled features, their dense, gleaming heads of hair which continued to decorate the tops of their high, intelligent foreheads even after they'd just emerged from intense lovemaking or fearless fistfighting, impressed Annabelle vividly, although the image which stayed stubbornly in her mind through book after book was that of Alan Alda, for some reason.

The breeze from the fan caressed Annabelle's bare backside while she turned the pages, her chin cupped in the palm of her free hand, that elbow propped on the mattress. Muted tones of sunlight glowed through the closed windows and lowered shades.

Like all girls who are conscious of their looks, Annabelle never forgot what parts of her body might be visible from various directions. Now, she could imagine what someone standing behind her would see – her silky-smooth thighs parted on the white sheets, small feet tucked under the carelessly thrown-back bedding her thighs, firm and smooth, tapering from her bottom toward the knees and calves, the two domes of her rump bulging up on their own, below her small waist, her sloping back half-hidden by her curtain of hair, the deep crevice between her cheeks curving down into her groin, disappearing inside her seductively concealed notch...

As soon as she thought about her cleft, she automatically pulled it inward, feeling it retract, the labia rolling tightly together as the lining of her cleft sucked into her body. She relaxed again, and at once her nervous feeling returned, making her skin prickle.

It's nobody, she insisted to herself.

She hadn't heard the door being opened or shut. There hadn't even been any sounds that she could hear from other rooms in the building. Only the distant noise of traffic on the boulevard beyond the park. It was as if the whole world was complying with Annabelle's private wish to be alone and undisturbed, so she could spend the slowly passing hours indulging in the pleasant pastime of daydreaming.

Then, why did she feel she was being watched, studied by a stranger, as if a Peeping Tom, by some miracle of wicked cleverness, had managed to scale the sheer wall below the bedroom windows, all the way up to the fourth floor, had then undone the forty-year-old cast-iron casement, opening it wide enough to slide into the room, without Annabelle noticing anything, then stealing swiftly and expertly across to the alcove containing the dressing vanity and mirror, next to the door, from which there was a clear view of her on the bed, something that could be taken in at leisure, like a farmer idly studying the rear end of one of his prize cows...

Enraged by this notion, Annabelle pulled her legs together and yanked her knees up, rolling onto her side, so she could turn and face the corner where she felt the intruder was lurking, her dark eyes sending daggers through the gently-moving air of the room.

"Who – ?!" she started to blurt. But the place was as empty as it had been all along. The walls returned Annabelle's stare with blank, plastery innocence.

Her nervousness puffing away in a pink burst, she giggled at her silliness, flinging her feet out toward the rolled-back bedsheets again and flopping flat onto her back, staring up at the ceiling.

Exposed now to the draft from the fan, the moisture from her conical breasts, flat stomach, and slightly mound-shaped mons began to evaporate, her skin cooling and drying nicely.

How fortunate she was, she thought inwardly, that she could enjoy a cool breeze in the privacy of her room without interruptions. Thank heavens for telephone-answering services, unlisted numbers, and ground-floor doormen...

Lying there, with the front of her crotch gaping in the direction of the whirring fan, Annabelle remembered the sex dream she'd had so often lately.

Closing her eyes, she wondered if it was something that most girls dreamed, whenever they started thinking about their bodies.

It began with the idea of an unidentified force sneaking up on her, something masculine. Why was it that everything about females was secret and internal? Nothing ever stuck out or intruded into the surrounding world. Instead, it all faced inward, or was full like a container, pregnant, ready to give forth. Her groin extended in and in, to warm concealed caverns, tunnels and grottoes in her body which she only knew about from talking with girlfriends as a teenager, and later with gynecologists during office examinations – but which she didn't dare try to reach on her own.

Her breasts jutted out, sure. But they were containers, too, and if she ever had a child, they would fill up with milk.

But the antagonist in her dream, the male thing which never seemed to be human, was the precise opposite of her femininity. It protruded in all directions, hard and sharp, angular and aggressive. And instead of being full, like her, it was empty and hungry. It wanted to penetrate, and take. Mostly, it wanted to invade her. It searched constantly, moving from side to side, seeking a way through Annabelle's instinctive defenses, her soft resistance, for a path that might lead into her core. She could feel its pressure against her body, pushing, prying. When it finally found her weakest spot, she knew that it wouldn't hesitate to thrust deep without warning, with awesome force, entering her.

This was always when she would feel the full wrenching impact of the dream, because it was impossible for her to turn the invader away, to keep it from piercing all the way through into her core.

She was helpless.

And it was this helplessness that she invariably found to be so erotic.

Sure enough, now, as the dream unfolded once more and overwhelmed her, she felt herself responding. She was small again, secretly aware of the holes leading into her body, trying to find why the act of satisfying her desires had always been so 'nasty' in the eyes of her straitlaced mother. She kept her eyes shut and paid no attention to the heat building up in her, inside the deepest twisting hollow spaces. She ignored the way her legs were spreading apart by themselves, the way her rump bulged down against the bedsheets, her whole pelvis expanding apart like a blossoming flower for the approaching male thing...

This time, the dream was more realistic than ever. Somewhere in the back of her mind, she knew that what she was doing on the bed was disgusting. She was displaying herself wantonly to the empty air, exhibiting herself with brazen boldness, her body gaping, the electric fan still blowing its soft breeze against her skin.

She imagined how she must look right now, like some sort of fat pale farm beast, grunting and swollen, pushing herself still wider, so that soon nothing would show from below the bed but a pink, disembodied, glistening female crotch, a flower of unfolded membranes as big as an easy chair, dominating the room.

The male invader reached toward her.

It touched her, like the cold, hard snout of a probing jungle python, prodding her flesh, feeling for her private openings.

It poked, inspected, maneuvered –

– And plunged.

It seemed like an eternity before Annabelle finally moved on the bed and came swimming up, breathless and trembling, out of the hot bubbling depths of her orgasm.

The warmth swirling through her body felt almost too good...as though she'd done something special to herself which had never been done before. Even masturbation with a vibrator at her best friend's apartment had never felt this good...

The next sensation which gripped her was the feeling that she was no longer alone.

There was someone else on the bed with her!

It was the male thing!

She jerked away, sat up, and twisted sideways to see who it was.

Something tightened in her throat. It was the hero of her daydreams, the man from all those romances, dark-haired, clean-faced, lying there on the other side of her bed smiling up at her with that old, familiar, knowing, cockeyed grin. This couldn't be real, a voice inside her screamed.

At the same moment she became aware that she could no longer feel the texture of the bedding underneath her skin, that, in fact, she hadn't been able to feel a thing since she'd awakened just now from her dream!

The man, whose sculptured body was naked, and whose pale coral-pink penis was only now softening and shrinking below his rippling loins, proceeded to sit up and step away from her without so much as another backward look. God, he has magnificent buns, she thought as she continued staring at him while he went to her closet and slid it open.

Sometime ago a male friend of Annabelle's, whom she had picked up at the airport upon his arrival in town on business, had left a suit here to be cleaned, and hadn't yet been back to pick it up. Now, the stranger took it out from where she'd been keeping it. He slipped into the pants without bothering with underwear, and the shirt, the tie, and the jacket. There were shoes as well, and socks, which he put on.

Annabelle opened her mouth to stop him, but suddenly a wave of fear swept over her. What if she spoke and nothing came out?

Why did she feel so unreal?

As casually as if he was leaving his own apartment to go out on the town, the man opened the door of the bedroom. Then he turned at the last moment and grinned at her. He gave her a quick wink, half-smiling, just the way she'd imagined that all the heroes in her romances might do.

Oh, please, she thought desperately, don't go so soon – ! She wished she could hold onto him.

From the bed she reached out with her hands.

The strange conviction came up in her mind, quite abruptly, that this delectable male apparition was no stranger after all...that he had in fact been here the whole time, that he'd been the invisible alien watching her a moment ago, searching her, preparing to plunge into her and steal something vital out of her for his own use. He looked so confident now that she came to the conclusion, without any further need for thinking about it, that he had succeeded.

What, she wondered, had he taken?

And then the door was shut.

Annabelle glanced down at her hands.

She couldn't see them!

Something was terribly wrong!

Climbing off the bed she crossed toward the mirror over her dresser and stared into it. In the glass, the bedroom was empty! Annabelle was invisible.

What had the alien taken from her?

Why, only her reality, that's all.

She had to get out! She had to find him, and figure out a way to get her physical substance back.

She was too young to go through the rest of her life as a ghost!

Rushing to the door, Annabelle lunged out with her hands to grab the knob and twist it, to pull the door open and begin her pursuit of the male thing which had raped her. As she touched the knob, her fingers fell through it.

The door itself, however, and the walls on both sides of it, remained solid to her touch, resisting her with supernatural impenetrability. At last the full, terrible impact of what had happened to her began to sink in. She was enclosed in this cube, trapped inside a space bounded by four walls, a floor and a ceiling, beyond whose confines lay a world in which she no longer even existed!

And she would remain trapped here, she realized, haunting this chamber and nowhere else, until the male alien who had taken from her the one thing which made her real came back, if he ever bothered to.

How long, she wondered, had he been imprisoned here himself, before he'd finally discovered that he could be free?

Screaming silently in the soundless room, Annabelle dropped to her knees, clawing without the slightest effect against the door she could no longer open.

The New-Realism Experiment

He was in a strange place when he awoke. He didn't know how he had gotten here.

The disorientation didn't go away when he opened his eyes. He was lying in his clothes, on a satin-upholstered divan, in a small room facing a pair of closed French doors with glass panels, covered by curtains. A glow of light was coming through the curtains, and the shadows of moving shapes. He could hear that there was some kind of activity going on beyond them.

He'd been to parties before, some at places owned by people he hardly even knew. He had even gotten too drunk at some of them to be allowed to drive his own car home.

An attack of vertigo seized him as he rose from the divan. He leaned against a nearby wall until the spinning stopped.

His mind remained a blank. He searched his memory but couldn't come up with any tangible information. Not even his name.

"This is ridiculous!" he told himself impatiently.

How could he have gotten that drunk? What had he been drinking?

He turned, staring around himself. Absolutely nothing about the room was familiar. It was as if he'd never knowingly been here before.

Damn! he thought. He had to get out of here!

The doors weren't locked. He opened them, pulled them wide. Light flooded in.

A cocktail party was going on in the next room.

It was elaborately decorated, filled with glamorous people. His eyes widened. A man was playing a piano in a far corner. Women in evening gowns of silk and lace, sequins and rhinestones, strolled elegantly from conversation to conversation, daintily holding cocktail glasses or cigarette holders.

The man with amnesia entered the room.

"Oh! Hello, Mr. Townes!" A man with a well-groomed mustache rushed up to him. "Are you feeling better after your rest?"

The two men stood looking at each other.

Was he really someone named Townes?

"I – " he stammered, "I guess so."

The man with the mustache looked him over. He was shorter than Townes, if that was his name, and had a bald spot on his head.

"Nasty crack you took on that banister," the shorter man said. A hand went across the top of Townes's head. "No lumps, though."

Townes pulled away, feeling his own head. "I'm perfectly all right," he insisted. "But what was I doing – " He indicated the doors. " – in there?"

"We thought you should lie down for a while."

"Paul! Darling!" came a woman's voice.

Townes turned. She was the most gorgeous woman he had ever seen. Her eyes were liquid gems set in a face of purest ivory. Her hips flared deliciously, and her waist was a delicate stem. She hurried up to him and took hold of his hands.

"Paul, I'm so glad you're all right! I was terribly worried. Come over here and sit down. Let me get you another cocktail."

She got him seated and rushed off.

The man with the mustache sat next to him.

"Uhh..." Townes, if that was his name, addressed the other man tentatively. "Who...who is she?"

The man grinned. "You mean you don't recall – ?"

Townes nodded.

"You mean...you've lost your memory?"

"I guess I have."

The man looked concerned and sympathetic. "Oh, I'm so terribly sorry! Must've been that rap on your head."

"It must have been."

"Well," he explained, "that lovely creature's name is Lady Sonya. And you know her very well. You brought her here tonight, as your guest."

Townes said, "Am I married to her?"

"Oh, heavens no! You're a bachelor, and very likely to remain so."

The woman named Lady Sonya was back soon with the drinks. She had blonde hair, and wore nothing but white, as though she had been expecting to be married.

And it took her no time to begin touching Townes, crooning to him, leaning against him, and finally kissing him with hot, wet urgency.

The man with the mustache moved politely away before Townes could break free from Lady Sonya long enough to ask him any more questions.

Judging by the woman's enthusiastic attempts at lovemaking, he had to be either devilishly handsome, or lavishly rich. Since he wasn't the first, it had to be the second.

He tried pushing her away, and arguing her out of being so amorous, but it was no good. Finally, under the pressure of her increasing enjoyment, he reluctantly gave in. Either this was actually happening, as his senses so abundantly told him, or he was having an extremely vivid dream. It was enormously pleasant to be admired so passionately by such a beautiful female, and he saw no harm in going along with it.

Lady Sonya said that she knew of a back room where they could be alone together in private. She got up with him, and led him toward an obscure door in a different corner, while he apologized to her for his damnable loss of memory.

"Dear me," she sympathized, turning to face him again. "Does it hurt much?"

He laughed at this, holding her hand, and they went inside. She closed the door, and after his eyes adjusted Townes noticed a rather large bed nearby. He also observed, rather abruptly, that Lady Sonya was helping him out of his clothes.

She was the next to disrobe. She did it slowly, with style and flair, and Townes, if that was his name, watched in delight. If she had looked beautiful fully clothed, she was spectacular naked. He had to compliment himself – he had obviously excellent taste in women. Apparently, he must be quite a worldly sophisticate, he told himself.

"Lady Sonya," he said, as she pulled him down onto the bed, "I can't remember a thing about us. Only what I've learned since waking just now, that my name seems to be Paul Townes and yours is Lady Sonya."

"Darling," she laughed, holding his head closer so she could kiss him, "you are a sad one. The man with the mustache is Waldo Pembroke, one of your best friends. This is his townhouse in Kensington."

"You mean...London?"

She nodded. "And as for you, you're a man of the world, a bon vivant. You're independently wealthy, you own numerous businesses both here, in America, and on the Continent. You're a fascinating person, a collector of fine art and other beautiful things, you're a world traveler, a recognized wit, a speaker at engagements...Why else would someone like me have taken such an interest in you?"

Townes was fairly amazed at himself.

They spent a delightful hour on the bed, reaffirming a love affair of undoubtedly long duration and great intensity, during which Townes learned what a magnificent and accomplished lover Lady Sonya was.

"You've told me yourself, many times," she sighed afterward, "that a man must take life by the scruff of the neck and ride it for all it's worth. Don't you remember?"

He shook his head.

"Those're your very words. Taste everything in life at least once, see everything, do everything. Otherwise it'll pass you by. No matter what it is, fighting in a little war somewhere, climbing a mountain, crossing a desert, defeating a band of barbarians – "

"Have I done all that?"

"Of course you have! And I've done half of it with you!"

It had to all be true, he mused. She even rummaged for evidence of his exploits, showing him magazines with pictures of someone who definitely looked like him. In one he stood over a dead elephant in Africa, with her at his side, a gigantic rifle crooked in his arm. In another he wore an elaborate native costume and was standing in front of a vast Oriental temple. In yet another he was at the wheel of a sailing yacht, somewhere in mid-ocean, surrounded by a crew of athletic man and golden-haired girls.

Giving himself over to this dreamlike reality, Townes fell back into Lady Sonya's arms.

There was a mighty crash out in the main room. A frightened moan swept through the assembled party guests. Lady Sonya jumped up, pushing Townes off, and climbed from the bed. Together, they hastily dressed, Townes barely having time to retie his shoes and check the pockets of his pants before she opened the door and practically shoved him out into the brilliance.

The man with the mustache, Waldo Pembroke, was there, his eyes wide with dismay.

"He's here!" he announced.

Lady Sonya gasped, clutching Townes's shoulders from behind.

"Who? Who's here?" asked Townes.

"Her husband, of course!"

"You've got to hide!" said Lady Sonya.

He whirled on her. "You never told me!"

"Darling! I keep forgetting you've lost your memory!"

"Quickly! This way!" Grabbing Townes by one hand, Pembroke tried to drag him across the room. But Lady Sonya got a grip on his other hand, and wouldn't let go, pulling him back toward her.

Townes was about to object to being involved in a tug-of-war between the two, when suddenly a man in a red hunting jacket towered over all three of them, his face florid, brandishing a huge gun.

"You! Townes!" he roared. "You swine! First you drive me out of business, ruin me financially! And now this!"

"Harold!" Lady Sonya said, trembling. "Be reasonable."

"So you thought you could steal my honor too, is that it! Take my wife from me? Make me a horned cuckold in the eyes of my friends?" He had apparently been drinking heavily. His face was a mass of perspiration and bulging veins, his eyes like road maps. He took clumsy aim, nearly point-blank, with the ponderous gun.

Pembroke and Lady Sonya immediately let go of Townes's arms.

"Take this!" said Lady Sonya, digging in a small white handbag. She pulled out a petite, nickel-plated, pearl-handled revolver and pushed it into Townes's right hand.

"Why shouldn't I kill you, Townes?" the big man boomed. "You've left me nothing worth living for!"

"He means it!" screamed Lady Sonya. "Use my gun! Now! Shoot him before he shoots you! It's his life or yours!"

All at once Townes felt his control slipping away.

"Shoot! Shoot!" bellowed Pembroke.

"Yes, go ahead, shoot!" said Harold. "I don't think you have the guts!"

If this was a dream, thought a buried part of Townes's mind, it had just now turned into a first-class nightmare. He couldn't remember ever having held a handgun before, or trying to aim it. Shivering, squeezing his eyes nearly shut, he raised Lady Sonya's gleaming pistol and fired.

The boom it made was out of all proportion to its small size.

Townes tried not to faint.

Somewhere in front of him, a large body tumbled onto the floor with a tremendous crash.

He dropped the pistol and opened his eyes in abject dread.

The big man lay face-down on the carpet, his own gun nearby, one hand outstretched toward it, in a slowly spreading lake of blood.

"You killed him," breathed Lady Sonya in amazement.

He turned to look at her.

To his shocked surprise her face was contorted with hate.

"You shot him!" she shrieked. "You murdered my husband!"

"But – !" he croaked.

"Lord Wemberley!" gasped Pembroke, kneeling next to the victim. "He's been shot all right. He's stone-dead."

The other guests milled around, staring with shocked expressions at Townes. "The assassin!" he could hear them muttering, the women backing away, the men surging closer. "Fiend! Savage! Monster!"

Townes tried to retreat from the gathering mob. They're all insane, he thought, in the grip of terror. None of this had been his decision. It had all happened without his consent. Lady Sonya had forced the gun into his hand, forced him to shoot! None of this could be real! He'd never killed anybody in his life!

Out of nowhere, the shrilling of police whistles split the air. Heavy fists pounded on a door at the other end of the room.

Grabbing him once again, Pembroke hustled him out the other way, toward a door that Townes hadn't noticed until this moment. The guests parted and watched him go, their eyes flashing fury at him. He permitted himself to be pulled along. Inwardly, he struggled to separate dream from reality, what he'd observed from what he believed. Was his name Townes? Had he ever known a woman named Lady Sonya? Was he a murderer? Was all of this merely some hideous joke?

He nearly fell through a dark vestibule, Pembroke shoving him roughly from behind. He felt something being shoved into a back pocket. Something else was pushed into his side pocket. At almost that same instant, the door at his back crashed shut. All light and sound were cut off totally, as if a switch had been thrown. The entire scene he'd just left became only a rapidly-fading vision.

He fought to recover his balance.

What he saw confirmed his strangest suspicions.

He was standing in the lobby of a quiet art gallery.

A liveried servant came up and handed him a printed card:

"You have just experienced what we like to call 'The New-Real-ism Experiment.' You paid to see it, and underwent mental conditioning to induce the proper state of mind. All the people you just saw were actors. None of what happened was real. Your memory, which was temporarily erased with the use of drugs, will return in a few minutes. You are in the lobby of the Regis Gallery. Your car is parked outside. Your keys, money, and identification are safe in your pockets. Thank you, and we hope you enjoyed our performance."

Santana Morning

Late at night, for the thousandth time, Randall Oliver came home to his cabin in the cool, dark, tree-shaded canyon, his dog trotting quietly alongside him. His backpack was loaded mostly with books. He came up the winding path, hearing the watery sound of the creek beside him, in the darkness.

Lights of other cabins along the way shone across the wet pebbles on the path, and sent starlike unexpected beams into his eyes through the leaves of the moisture-laden trees. A scent of green moss filled the air, and every time he took a breath he let out the dry, dusty weariness from hiking all day through these hills, above the sea of suburbs that lay far off in the distance past the ridges. Here in the moist darkness, he took in a deep lungful of a different melancholy.

Most of all, what he felt was loneliness.

He knew he would rather live here than anywhere. And yet nothing could change the underlying sadness he felt, from being so much by himself. Some days were better than others, of course. When mist from the ocean formed a featureless gray lid over these canyons, which the sun could not penetrate, the bitterness inside him welled up worse than ever, and set him to hour upon hour of woeful pondering. On days like this nothing seemed worth doing any longer, ambitions and desires became pointless, and even the dog no longer gained any pleasure from the occasional rabbit or squirrel he could chase.

He'd never experienced love. All his life he had known girls, and later women, and they had smiled at him and taken his hand, and led him to dances or parties, where he had given a little of himself. But only a little. For what he always did, what he seemed compelled to do, was play a false role, being happy or smart, or over-witty, until they simply gave up trying to communicate and drifted away.

It happened every time. Someone he wanted desperately to share himself with would turn, lay her hands on his, or ask to be touched, her eyes and her lips would smile, and an invisible wall of shyness would rise to shut her off.

He could almost see the barrier go up. He often wondered that nobody else heard the busy rumble of its swift construction, the sudden and complete blocking-out. Every time, without exception, he became a prisoner of himself.

And then he was another man, loud and cruel, using too many vicious words. He hurt the girls, without wanting to, and they turned sadly away from him to find companionship elsewhere.

He often remembered the few girls who had tried to change him, so long ago. They had stayed with him despite his efforts to discourage them, to throw them off. They gave him attentions and gifts, tried especially hard to break through his shell. He still had many of their gifts, bottles of cologne and bits of jewelry, trinkets aglitter in tiny boxes, and he treasured them. But those many years ago, he had insulted and ignored these girls as well, until even the most determined of them had departed.

Randy could still recall some of their names, and said them now and then to himself, reciting them like poetry, whenever he felt so lonely.

He'd left his former life in the city long ago, the world of offices and business suits, appointments and lunches with clients. He had given that up when he moved out here, finding this canyon in the brush-covered hills. By then, almost thirty years of his life had leaked by without his tasting so much as a kiss, or hearing the words, 'I love you,' sincerely spoken by a feminine voice.

Back in that other world, the urban life had been a brutal game of searching, where the winners walked off with the girls while the losers went home to their empty rooms and hollow lives alone. He'd had a career in the city, though he could hardly remember what it had been.

And now his only companion, the wrinkle-faced mongrel, kept him company on his nightly return to the cabin by the stream. His relationship with the dog had been spontaneous and mutual. They had each realized that they needed the other.

Now, in his cabin, the yearning and the dreams lingered while Randy busied himself about the small, enclosed room. He lit his gasoline lantern, put away his things, and fed the dog.

It bothered him like the clammy dampness left in his narrow bunk by the weeks of canyon mists, and stayed with him like the breathing, scratching dog who walked around a tight circle before settling onto his accustomed bed. It echoed in the unusual strength of the sometime-running creek outside the single open window, the gurgling rock-rattling liquid conversation mingling with the rustle of leaves over the roof, as the darkness covered him softly, lowering him easily, to sleep.

It was from a dream of warmth and touching, of soft words and closeness, that Randy woke abruptly, to an awareness of wind.

There was a thrill in the air. Tree branches danced outside his window. The leaves glowed as brilliantly as new toys, lit from beyond by the white, clean-scrubbed sun. The air that came in through the screen to fill the cabin was no longer clammy with sea moisture, but dry as clean rocks and sagebrush.

This was the Santa Ana, or as Randy had always preferred to call it, the Santana. It was a desert wind from the other side of the mountains above this canyon. To many people it was a fire wind, a devil wind, a dangerous invader bringing only trouble. But to him it meant freedom and change.

It made him want to be up and about, dressed and on his way, excited to see where it was going and if he could go along with it.

The dog, who had already been out enjoying the morning, came loping back to see if Randy was ready to go exploring. Randy stepped outside as soon as he could.

The creek was running clear, splashing over rock ledges. If this wind kept up for long enough, it would shrink to a trickle. The canyon was alive with moving tree shadows. Sunlight shining between the shifting branches mottled his arms and decorated his jacket with patterns. Later today, he realized, it would probably be hot enough for him to hike up to the pool under the waterfall, at the head of the canyon. Maybe he would meet others there too.

The wooden cabins along the path glowed with bright, new, golden-sienna colors under the clear sky. The doors of those which were inhabited stood open, their occupants moving around outside, like the dog, each one savoring their first taste of the new-minted world.

Randy felt an unexpected presence, close by his side. He turned and found himself looking down into the face of a girl.

For a moment he couldn't seem to focus his eyes on her. She was a blur, featureless and indistinct. He blinked, then stared at her again.

"Hi," she said, in a soft, clear voice.

"Hello."

He suddenly saw her, sharp and distinct. She had fiery copper-red hair and large, washed-out, grayish-blue eyes. She wore heavy, scuffed hiking boots, a long-sleeved orange sweatshirt, inside-out, several sizes too large, and faded, skin-tight blue jeans.

The man hadn't spoken to anyone for so long that he now considered words to be precious.

He chose carefully the ones he wanted to say.

"Who are you?"

She stepped closer. "Who do you want me to be?"

Her evasion startled him.

"Do you have a name?"

"I have many names."

She reminded him of T. S. Eliot's poems about cats, how every cat had three names, the public one, the personal one, and the secret one.

"What is your favorite name?" he asked.

She shuffled her feet for a moment on the gravel, which this morning was no longer damp. "I don't know," she said at length. "There are so many. There is Wind, and Springtime, and Joy. Clear Water, Cool Surf, and Desert Sunset. You could call me Citrus, or Spice, or Relish, and I would turn to answer. If you stood and shouted for Fair Breeze, Caressing Mist, White Dove or Bright Sunshine, I would head toward you at once, happy that you knew me."

The man was more beriddled than ever.

"May I call you an ordinary name instead?"

She laughed, a tinkling clarity of sound.

"How about Andrea?" he said. "I used to know a girl named Andrea, who looked a lot like you." He refused to tell her that this other Andrea had once begged to let her marry him.

"Isn't that a coincidence!" she said, laughing again.

He looked at her. "What?"

"That happens to be my name. Andrea! How about that!"

She moved past him, the closeness of her shapely, rounded body sending thrills of agitation through him.

"This cabin," she said, leaning forward to peer inside, through the open doorway. "Is it yours? Is it where you live?"

"Yes." It was almost a shamefaced confession.

The dog bounded up on her other side. Andrea turned, stooped, and reached to touch him, which made the dog edge closer, his mouth hanging open in the nearest expression he had to a smile, brown eyes sparkling, pink tongue lolling.

"Is he yours too?"

"Uh-huh." He moved aside. "Would you like to come in and sit down?"

"Sure."

"You must be tired," he said, "and hungry. And thirsty. Want a cup of coffee? Want something to eat?"

"That would be nice."

Randy went to get creek water for the coffeepot. Climbing back to the cabin, he tried not to think about what it was like to have a girl inside, not wanting to dwell on where she'd come from, or how she'd managed to suddenly come into his life.

Not looking at her, he came in through the open doorway and lit the stove. Putting the coffee on, he reached sideways, got his frying pan, and made a breakfast of his last eggs and half of his bread, frying the toast with butter in the pan. He poured steaming coffee, and set down a plate in front of Andrea.

As she began to eat, he pulled over a stool from the opposite corner and sat looking across the table at her. Andrea reminded him of the deer and squirrels who occasionally appeared outside his door, nervously seeking a leftover morsel. She peered forward at him with dark, oversized eyes while she ate, as though at any moment she would raise her head, turn away, and disappear as suddenly as she had come.

Then she smiled. And the old sensations returned, ones he hadn't felt in years. He was faced with undeniable reality, the way one is faced with the street outside a movie theater, when it is evening, the lights are on, and you thought it was still afternoon, after a particularly long and engrossing show.

Are you a dream, he wanted to ask her, or are you real?

What he finally did ask her was, "Where are you from?"

"Does it matter?" She took another bite of toast. "Where would you like me to be from?"

She was playing an enigmatic game. Did she want him to construct her past, give it to her, fact by fact? Was she a blank form, like the outlines in an unused coloring book? Was she challenging him to fill those outlines in?

He realized that he wanted to play. It was something he had wanted to do for a long time.

"You're from back east," he said.

She smiled. He went on. "You've been traveling across the country. You've been hitchhiking, trying to get to the coast. You ran away from home."

"You know all about me," she said.

"You grew up in a very small town, which had strict rules about how people were supposed to behave. Your childhood was very sad. Your parents were overprotective, especially your father. He kept you away from people, not allowing you to make friends. He did it because he loved you, but he made you feel like a prisoner, nevertheless."

"It's a sad world," she said. "I'm sorry you have to hear about my troubles. I shouldn't burden you with them."

He shook his head. "That's all right. I enjoy learning about people."

The wind blew outside the cabin, pushing against the wooden walls. Tree leaves whispered in a thousand separate voices.

"I've been alone for a long time," he said.

She finished her eggs and sat back in the chair, her eyes searching his.

"Tell me more about myself."

He took a breath. "You've been hurt by people you hoped would help you. You thought they loved you, you even tried to get them to love you, and they let you down. Strangers have taken advantage of you. It's been going on for years."

It was as though he could see her with increasing clarity while he spoke. The pale form kept changing, taking on color and texture, substance, weight, presence, until a real girl sat in front of him. A strand of her hair dangled over one eye.

"You wanted to be an artist, didn't you," he said. "You were good at drawing and painting while you were in school."

"Yes," she said passionately. "Oh, yes."

"But you still couldn't convince your father, even when your teachers tried to tell him about your talent, when you were offered scholarships to art schools in other cities. He wouldn't let you go. He was too afraid for you."

"Daddy was so scared for me," she said. "One night I actually caught him crying, as he sat at the dining-room table, after the rest of us had all gone to our rooms."

"So you finally left. You had just enough money for a bus ticket. You took the bus to a city where one of your teachers had said there would be a job waiting for you. But when you got there you discovered that your boss was only interested in using you. That was when you started hitchhiking."

She nodded.

"Along the way, men did things for you, as long as you played along."

"Do you despise me for giving in to them?"

He shook his head. "It's what you had to do." By now, he knew Andrea intimately, every feeling, every memory, every need and desire, every accomplishment, each private victory. She was part of him, an extension of his own soul. He and she were connected to each other, related.

"Does it bother you that I ran away from home, that I didn't appreciate all the things that Daddy was trying to do for me?"

"No," he said. "And don't be bitter. You're safe now, as long as you're here with me. I won't try to hold onto you, though. If you want to leave, I'll let you go." He looked at her. "Only, I'm so thrilled that you're here, that you've showed up so unexpectedly, almost as if the wind brought you here, that I hope and pray you won't want to leave too soon."

The light outside slanted upward, shifting nearer to noontime.

Andrea's eyes still held the same enchantment. He felt responsible for her. He had conjured her out of his longing. He had created her! But that couldn't be right. He could reach across and touch her. She could push him away if she wanted. But she didn't. As he touched her hand, she brought her other hand over and laid it on top of his.

Then she stood up, stretched, and yawned.

"I'm tired. I could use some sleep."

"Go ahead, take my bunk."

After she'd gone to sleep, he stepped outside and gently closed the cabin door.

The wind surrounded him as he wandered up the gravel path. It came streaming down off the mountain, melting the high snows to fill the creek. His dog galloped toward him out of the weeds and turned to dash off again, his ears flying. When the dog returned, he dug his fingers affectionately into the fur on his neck.

The joy from the strange new thing that had happened this morning made him want to rise up and fly into the high, clear blue above the trees. He kept seeing everything around him as if it had never existed before. A marvelous intensity of joy filled him. He had a girl in his cabin! The fact of it astounded him. It made him jump and stamp his feet in the rushing air. He, who had given up women and moved away to avoid them now had a genuine, real, wonderful one of them in his cabin, sleeping on his bunk, resting her lovely head on his pillow.

With the dog racing ahead, he ran up the canyon, alongside the creek. Reaching the upper end, where the sun minted the rock walls a rich, mellow gold, he stood facing the waterfall, which was running spectacularly today, with the full force of fresh water. It surged over a rim, far up against the sky, dropping into a deep, perfect turquoise pool at the bottom.

The day was already warm enough for the dog to go splashing happily into the pool. As he watched, the man sat down, took off his heavy shoes, pulled up the legs of his pants, and waded away from the shore.

On his way back to his cabin, a single thought plagued him.

Would his inner walls of mistrust and shyness shoot invisibly up once again, guarding his privacy, shutting Andrea out?

Would he end up hurting her, the way others had hurt her?

God, he thought, I hope I don't wound her! I hope I can't. She's my second chance! I never want to make her cry. If I did I could lose her! I mustn't drive her away!

Reaching his cabin, late that afternoon, he opened the door. A stray sunbeam filtered through the wind-fluttering leaves across the way, sending its light into the doorway.

A fresh thrill surged through him. Andrea hadn't been a dream. She was still there, her blonde hair shining, asleep on his bunk.

Had the old days been that different? Was he so much less vulnerable now? Was he that much changed, had living out here by himself taught him so much that was new?

Why did this girl, and only this one, bother him so little? Was Andrea such a contrast with all her predecessors?

He asked himself these questions many times over the following two days, while the wind continued to blow. He asked them each night when he went to sleep beside her in the cabin, hearing the small noises she made while she slept, aware of her lying only inches away from him in the dark.

But the answers didn't actually matter. The barrier was down, he still had Andrea there, and she still liked being with him. That was enough, that the girl and he were together.

Dreams rushed to reality. Randy saw them being fulfilled, flooding out into daylight in the form of hands, arms, eyes, long silky hair. They shaped themselves into Andrea, radiant in the afternoon, with a fur of tiny hairs on her skin that stood out in the sun when she stood between him and shadow.

It was twenty years of private, secret wishing coming true all at once, in a rush. It left Randy feeling dizzy with the power of their happening. She didn't leave. Not that afternoon, or even the following morning.

Together, they sat by the creek and listened to it. To have her there beside him was amazing. It made him feel wonderful, not being alone any longer. Andrea was vibrantly alive, turning her head, aware of everything. She led him down to the creek and scooped up a double handful of the clear, cold water, drinking some herself, and offering the rest to him.

He spent most of his time with Andrea simply talking. She told him more and more about herself. And it seemed that every new thing she said, he already knew. She was tired of hitchhiking, she said, and wanted to stay somewhere and listen to the silence of the world, in a place where leaves rustled softly in the clear air, birds sang and animals moved in the undergrowth. The air smelled good here, made spicy with growing things.

Randy got himself another sleeping bag from one of his neighbors down the trail. He unrolled it on the cabin floor every night, next to the bunk, and slept close beside his dog, where he could listen to the gentle rhythm of Andrea breathing.

Then, when the wind was still blowing, keeping the sky as clear as an open eye and pushing the damp cold of the mist-shrouded evenings away, he took Andrea with up the trail, to the top end of the canyon, so he could show her the waterfall.

There was a blue-green pool below the roaring white cataract. In the brilliance, under the pastel canyon walls, they sat and listened to the roar of the water, watching the interplay of highlights below.

"I've never been so happy," said Andrea. She clutched Randy by the arm, holding onto him and resting her head on his shoulder as they sat on the small, sloping beach with their shoes off, dipping their bare feet into the crystal water.

The barriers inside Randy's mind hadn't come down to block off this girl. He was able to live freely with her, talking with her, sharing himself without feeling the obligation to put on a false show of himself. It was a dream he'd never had before. He was relaxed with her, able to put his arm around her and rest his hand on her skin, and not feel self-conscious or embarrassed.

"I have so much to thank you for," she told him. The waterfall thundered into the pool. A hushed rain of spray settled softly around them. "I think you're wonderful," she said.

There were silent touchings and probings after that, not needing words, having sufficient accompaniment in the music of wind and water. She felt so perfect in his arms, warm and real. All at once their lips met and they were kissing.

"I love you," he heard himself say, as if he was hearing it from a stranger.

Later, when sunlight slanted near the ridge and lit up a chapel-full of stained-glass sycamore leaves from behind, the two of them walked back down the canyon to Randy's cabin. Flecks of gold dust floated on the suddenly-still air, and the stream, where it was crossed by a footbridge, was a flood of diamonds and ice.

Each knew what would come next, once they reached the cabin and stepped inside. Without discussing it, they had decided how they would undress, then lie on the bunk, how their bodies would fit.

He saw the way the sunlight settled in her hair, making it shine against the shadows. He saw her hands and legs, the soft flap of her skirt against her thighs as she walked beside him. He noticed her blouse, and the twin softnesses underneath, shaped for touching.

He held her tender hands in his.

She eyed him with the nervous eagerness of a doe, eyes wide and liquid, asking only for politeness.

They were at the cabin, then inside, and sitting side by side on the bunk.

"I love you," he repeated.

"I'm happy for you," she responded.

"How desperately I've wanted you...!"

At the end of a long hesitation, while rays of sun illuminated parts of the room and parts of Andrea through the moving screens of leaves outside, she stood up, stretched like a cat, and began undoing her blouse. Randy watched, seated, his hands amazingly clammy with the anticipation he felt. She looked down at him, her eyes overflowing.

She stood where the sun came in through the doorway, filtered to a rich greenness, and undressed especially for him. He saw her body being slowly, lovingly revealed, as she gave him her secrets like presents, one by one.

When the final truth hit, it was a quaking jolt of shock to Randy, and brought the whole wonderful dream crashing in around him.

"No!" he shouted, eyes averted, jumping to his feet. "No, Andrea, it's impossible. Stop it! Stop!"

He was close to weeping as he forced her to put her clothes back on, and then forced her to pack her things.

"But, darling," she faltered, "but..."

He held her by her tiny shoulders. "You're only a kid," he told her.

"I'm sorry I ever thought about it, Andrea. I wanted something I couldn't have anymore. You're young enough to be my daughter. I'm an old man!"

He got her belongings for her, the few she'd brought, then handed her the suitcase at the door. "I want you to go. I'll help you down to the bottom of the canyon, where you can catch the bus into the city. I'm no good for you. It's too late for me. I'm no good for anybody anymore. I thought I was, but it was just a dream."

Tears were beginning at the corners of her eyes. "But Randy," she breathed, "that's why I came! You needed me!"

"Don't fool yourself," he said, towing her determinedly down the path past the other cabins, as dusk gathered under overhanging branches. "I don't need anybody."

"But...but you *know* me! Intimately! You know everything about me, everything you told me about myself. We created ourselves for each other!"

When he still refused to relent, she said, "I found you at your cabin when the wind started, and now I have nowhere else to go! I have no home, nothing but this." She held up the suitcase. "I've got nobody but you. What'll I do in the city?"

"How about your girlfriend? Go to her, stay with her, and have her take you to meet some of her friends."

She went on with him, into the thickening night, down the path to the highway. And when they arrived at the side of the road, next to a combination diner and gas station, they stopped and waited for the bus. She begged him, one last time, to let her stay with him. She wept, held onto him, beat at his chest with her fists when he thrust her away again.

Finally she blurted, "You can't make me go! I'm a part of you." She accused him with her contorted face, a fierce mixture of tears and anger in the half-light. "It was you who made me! Damn it, Randy, don't you understand? I'm your creation!"

"That's a lie," he replied hoarsely. "I don't believe it. I'll never believe it. You're real as real can be."

"Oh, am I?" she challenged. "You made me up out of your dreams! You wanted another chance, and there I was! You dreamed me up, Randy, *you dreamed me up!*"

And he saw her features starting to melt, change, flow down into an overall paleness, a blank form, a coloring-book outline once again. In a moment he couldn't even recognize her.

The bus was there, its engine idling noisily under the trees, between the looming hills on both sides of the road. He paid the fare to the driver, and turned away. He didn't know her, had never known her. She'd been only a dream.

He started back up the path to his cabin.

Had she vanished? He suddenly found that he was silently weeping. All the way to his cabin, the tears continued flowing silently down his face.

The dog came trustingly along with him.

His thoughts raged. How intensely he had wanted Andrea! No physical want could have been greater. He didn't want the talk or the friendship, or even the love, of a girl. He wanted more, something deeper, that he could feel with his soul along with touching it with his fingers. His desire was there still, barely beyond feeling. His fingertips ached, his heart pulsed, his arms throbbed with the longing.

But the Andrea he wanted wasn't to be found. She was the reflection, in the back of his mind, of long-ago times when he'd been a young man, and could take his pleasure in the love of women. He wanted too much from Andrea. He wanted to name her, even, and select her past. He wanted to shape her, mold her, transform her into his personal ideal, despite what might really have been.

That depended, of course, on whether she'd actually ever been real.

He had wanted everything from her, love as well as companionship. Possession. Ownership and the right to change her at will. And she had been willing, so willing to give him whatever he'd wanted! And he wasn't even capable of taking it!

He wanted, in the final analysis, the return of his youth. He wanted to be able to love Andrea, in the same way that he had always wanted to love a real flesh-and-blood woman. He'd counted on too much with Andrea, and now he knew it.

It was once again very late at night, for the thousandth time, and he was returning to his cabin in the cool tree-lined canyon, with the wetly running creek in the darkness to one side of the gravel trail.

Lights of the other cabins still sent their beams piercing through the shadows, and onto the pebbles so that they shone like jewelry, casting inky shadows toward him.

His friendly wind, his Santana, had died away. It was as though everything in the last two days had never happened at all.

He stepped into his cabin and took out a kitchen match to light the lantern on the table. The mists had cooled the night air so that the bunk and the small wooden room around it were filled with a sort of sadness, a feeling of loss, loneliness, and unfulfilled yearning.

The anguish followed him into his narrow, solitary bed, and stayed with him while he went to sleep, like the breathing dog who curled around alongside him and dropped to the floor with a sigh. His dreams were there once again, and led him softly, gently downward, into darkness.

The City

Howard 388 stood at the top of the Town Spire in Middlebury, Nevada, looking down at the vast city below. It was sometime after midnight, and the observation level of the spire was unoccupied. The day had been dry and hot, and even this long after sundown, heat still radiated from the surface under Howard's feet. The lights of Middlebury and the surrounding suburbs extended off toward the far-distant horizon.

For a brief moment, Howard admired the view.

But he had another reason for being here. He was tired of trying so hard just to live another day. He wanted to end the struggle here and now. The top of the Town Spire was a good place for that. It was a mile high.

Of course, nobody committed suicide that way anymore. Howard knew he was being melodramatic, and what the city masters would call 'messy' on their television tirades, which went on most of the time. The Suicide Centers were clean, comfortable, efficient, even painless, and they were open 24 hours a day.

Howard hated the mass attitudes toward suicide. The population explosion hadn't been his fault. He was 35 years old now, and he hadn't even been near a girl yet, except for strictly controlled social functions. Normal sex between men and women had been declared illegal roughly a hundred years ago. The world was simply too full of people.

Nowadays, you had to get a license, find the girl, and talk her into consenting. And Howard hadn't yet figured out how to find the girl. The sexes were kept strictly separate.

Besides, there were lots of other things to do. And Howard, to pass the time, had tried most of them. There was Auto Racing, where to win a prize you climbed into super-powered gasoline racers with no safety devices, and raced on a quarter-mile indoor track, the driver who survived the longest being the winner. There was Bull Fighting, where you and a dozen other contestants stepped out into an arena facing a live bull, and the winner was the one who could use as many of his partners as possible as human shields on the horns. There was also Murder, where for a small fee you could hunt down a consenting enemy and slaughter whoever it turned out to be in any way that you saw fit, unless your enemy slaughtered you first.

Howard had been to the all-male dances, the social bathing, the nude Olympics for gentlemen, and the organized-sadism clubs. He had spent evenings at the Satan Society, afternoons at the Count Marquis Wrestling and Massage Parlor, and weekends with Fellows' Fellowship at their beach camp. But all these acceptable pleasures, which normally took his mind off mating, had had no effect lately on Howard's most pressing urge.

He wanted a woman.

He knew it was impossible. He had even signed up for blind dating, but by his latest calculations he was forty years back on the waiting list. By the time his turn came up, and he could finally walk into the dormitories and meet a real girl, he knew he would be too old to mate at all. Unless he was extremely lucky, and his application was speeded up. But Howard had learned not to trust luck. So it was impossible.

But he was still a man, and still relatively young. He needed the love of a girl. And he needed it now, while he could give a woman satisfaction.

On the observation level, Howard leaned over the railing and peered sadly down into a mile of empty space. He choked back a sob, as he'd caught himself doing so often lately.

Then something startled him, and he straightened again.

Someone stood beside him.

He turned and looked.

It was a girl.

She was plain, with a long doleful face and large, moist eyes. She had long, stringy hair, hanging from under a floppy hat. Her clothes were drab and worn, and had been washed too many times. The numbers of a female dormitory were stenciled on the shoulder of the jacket, and one leg of the pants.

She swung her eyes sideways, returning Howard's look.

He was suddenly ecstatic. His grief vanished. She was a female. And she was real! This was no fantasy. She didn't need to be beautiful, or even pretty. Just being a girl was enough.

"Howard is my name," he blurted, extending a hand.

"Angela," she said. They shook hands.

"That's a nice name."

He looked closer. Her cheeks, he noticed, glistened in the dimness. She'd been weeping.

"My name isn't going to matter in only a moment," she said. "I came up here – "

" – To jump?" he said.

Her eyes widened. "You too?"

He nodded. "But now you're here! Did you come up here because you were tired of trying to get a Mating permit?"

She edged shyly toward him. "Yes," she said breathlessly.

"I'm here for the same reason."

"It was so late when I finally managed to sneak away from my dormitory," she said, "that I thought I'd be alone."

They both grinned. It felt good to feel so happy all of a sudden. Howard knew that he hadn't smiled in years.

"But we aren't alone, are we," he said. "And if you're thinking what I'm thinking – !" He unbuttoned his coat.

"It's a warm night," she responded. "What better place?"

She began taking off her clothes, too.

Journey by Heliodrome

There didn't seem to be anything unusual about the little man with the mustache, in the brown three-piece pinstripe suit, with the bowler hat, standing at the edge of the railroad platform. Nor were there any anomalies about what he had on the display behind him, on his wooden horse-drawn wagon.

Which was why Alfred turned and wandered off in that direction.

He had been traveling alone, by train, crossing lonely country late in the year. Icy winds whipped his coat as he strode across toward the little man's merchandise.

He felt lost, homeless, even though he was homeward bound. His weariness seemed incurable. Something irresistible called to him from the wagon. He felt the last of his money aching to be spent on a cure for his melancholy.

The wagon's owner, a small-town Midwestern hawker, smiled in the gloom of the overcast, and stepped forward. "Hello there, stranger. Something I can do for you?" He came forward, took Alfred's shoulder, swung him around, and escorted him back toward his goods.

Alfred didn't answer, but instead proceeded to pore soberly over the garish aggregation. Such an array of multicolored items stood out starkly on such a gray day, almost as if they were aglow with an inner light.

Alfred stared at the florid trinkets, bits of statuary, Japanese paper parasols, flags, bonnets, books, magazines, fireworks and secondhand men's apparel he saw being offered for sale. Handpainted neckties, photos of Little Egypt at the Chicago Exposition, and genuine guaranteed Mexican jumping beans caught his attention.

And then there was the heliodrome.

He reached forward over the other items to touch it, as if to convince himself it was real, and the salesman immediately knew Alfred's look.

"So you found something, hey, son?" he said, and pushed in on Alfred's flank. "Here, just a minute..." He got hold of the thing, and lifted it grandly free of its encroachment of oddities, holding it high.

"It's a heliodrome."

Alfred's voice was uncertain as he said, "...a heliodrome?"

"A heliodrome," the pitchman repeated. "A pleasant gadget. Invented by a bicycle mechanic in Peoria. A sort of toy, you might say. An afternoon diversion." His mustache did a little twitch.

"What does it do?" Alfred asked.

"Why," the man explained, "it flies. Or so they say." He rotated the rubber-coated rotor blade atop its metal shaft. Alfred knew immediately that he wanted to buy it.

"How...how much is it?"

"Well – " the man said, hesitating. "How much were you considering?"

Alfred took out his wallet.

"I've only got...five dollars..." he said slowly, "to last me till I get home."

"I'll let you have it for four-fifty."

Alfred looked the contraption over slowly. It was small and lightweight, apparently made to be worn on the back. The gearbox was operated by a crank, and, in turn, it operated the shaft, to which the rotor was attached over the head, like a beanie-propeller. The blade looked like two canoe paddles dipped in latex.

Behind him, the locomotive chuffed anxiously, hissing steam. A bell clanged, the conductor hollered 'Aboard!' and passengers could be heard coming across the platform and re-entering the cars.

"Better hurry, son," said the hawker. "It appears your train's leaving."

Alfred dug into his wallet. "I'll take it."

He counted out four dollars and fifty cents, with hurried glances over his shoulder at the train. He handed over his money, and the salesman handed him the heliodrome. Around him, a colder wind whipped at his overcoat. The heliodrome's blades rotated.

The train whistle blew insistently, and the train clanked on the rails, pulling away from the platform.

"Want a receipt?" the salesman asked.

"Thank you, no!" Alfred said hastily, and sprinted for the departing train, heliodrome in hand.

"Glad to be of service!" the man called behind him.

The train was moving too fast now for Alfred to catch up. He ran a wide circle of the platform, pursuing it until the hopelessness of his effort finally halted him. He stood watching the train until it was out of sight, pondering his next course of action. His baggage was gone, and most of his money.

But still he had the heliodrome.

"The heliodrome!" he cried suddenly, and held it up.

The pitchman stood by his wagon, watching.

Alfred changed his hold on the heliodrome, so he could turn the crank. The gearbox whirred, the rotor spun with a beating sound, and a considerable gust of air shot down, so that it tugged itself upward, almost out of his grasp. The pull reminded him of the way a rowboat would move when you pulled with all your strength on the oars.

"Of course," he shouted jubilantly. "I'll *fly* home!"

The pitchman approached him. "You'll what?"

Alfred turned to face him. "I'll *fly* home," he said.

"But that thing's just a toy."

"You said that one could fly with it."

The gentleman held his chin. "Yes," he admitted. "But that's only hearsay. This is the only one I've ever seen, and I've never personally done any flying with it."

Alfred was strapping on the device. He tightened the chest strap, and the shoulder straps. The other man watched, momentarily silent.

"The fellow who sold it to me," he said at length, "made only three of them, for his own children."

Alfred turned the crank, and the rotor whipped around with a great deal of force. "It seems like it *has* to work! Feel that draught!"

The hawker held out a hand. There was quite a wind.

"And I can feel it lifting," Alfred said.

He rotated the crank with more authority, and, as the hawker watched, he began to rise. He looked exactly like a scarecrow or a preacher, so unusually lanky and sharp-edged in his flapping greatcoat and trousers. And now, his face was reddened, his eyes squinted with effort, his teeth gritted as he cranked. He was a strange bat-like scarecrow standing at the very center of the railroad-station platform, making a *thwop-thwop-thwop*ping sound with the whirligig above his head. It was like a halo over him, and he could scare hordes of crows or convert crowds of hopeful penitents with it. He rose only slightly at first, on tiptoes. But then, as the draught grew in strength, and the rotors whirred more swiftly, his feet cleared the boards and he was airborne. The pitchman stepped back in amazement, seeing an impossibility. Alfred floated two feet above where he'd stood before!

And then he dropped gently down again.

"Yep," he said breathlessly, "I'll fly home with this."

"How far from here is that?" the pitchman asked.

"Oregon."

"But Oregon's at least a thousand miles west of here!"

"It's not far, if you fly," Alfred reasoned.

The gentleman clucked his tongue. "Well, I just watched you do it. If you're serious about this, you had better take along something to eat, when you get hungry. Wait right here." He hurried back to his wagon and fumbled in the luggage boot up front.

Upon his return, he presented Alfred with a paper sack. "Sandwiches," he said. "And some fruit."

"I really shouldn't."

"Go ahead," the pitchman urged, smiling. "My wife always packs too much. They're Swiss cheese and ham. She thinks I'm too skinny."

Alfred took the lunch, and thanked the man, packing it inside his coat. Slapping his sides, he grinned. "I'm ready, I guess."

He gripped the crank again, and gave it a turn.

The salesman stepped back. "Good luck!"

Alfred waved back at him, cranking. Then he checked his feet, and looked around once at the station, the trees, and the leaden sky.

The heliodrome felt warm and comfortable on his back. The straps caressed him securely. A stiff breeze blew down from the whirling rotors.

He bore down on the crank. The little gearbox sang like a living thing, a companion, and the blades chopped more powerfully at the air, biting through it, flailing inexorably, creating a distinctive lift.

The straps gripped him ever more firmly, and the mechanism pulled him steadily skyward. Alfred momentarily realized with delight how proficient he already was with the little crank. It was easy! He eased off a bit, and looked down for the first time.

The ground was far below him!

In a circle of trees, the astounded pitchman stared almost straight up at him, doll-like on the station platform, next to a toy wagon below one edge, with a tin-soldier horse. The railroad depot was a gingerbread cake, candy-decorated, and he had an urge to feel around for an electric control to the model railroad. He waved with his free hand. The hawker, mouth agog, held up a pale hand and waggled it.

"It works!" yelled Alfred.

He decided to gain more altitude, and put more gusto into his cranking. He saw the countryside drop still further underneath his feet. He climbed speedily, above treetops, hills, birds and horizons. As he watched, whole new vistas opened up in all directions. A blackbird circled him for a moment, crowing, and he waved calmly at it.

He could see for miles. The entire valley was laid out beneath him, and he could see the town around the depot, all together, like a paper city on a tabletop. Streets and blocks were a checkerboard quilt on the lumpy ground. But he could no longer see the pitchman. He was far too high up for that, with a great gulf of nothing below, emptiness and silence.

Alfred relaxed, cranking along, with only a lolling flutter accompanying his reverie.

When he inadvertently leaned forward, he shot ahead like a bullet, until he kicked forward again, thrusting himself upright. This was a new effect, and he spent some time experimenting with it, turning and leaning this way and that, until he could streak off at any angle, in any direction, and stop himself or change his course at will. He swooped and soared with his heliodrome, crossing and recrossing the town and its environs.

He paced a few birds, and dove toward a field beside a chicken hawk. At the last minute, he kicked backward, and shot out in low-level flight, clearing a fence by inches and rustling the leaves of the farmer's trees.

Moments later, he'd caught up with his train. It raced with mechanical stubbornness for the mountains, clanking and clattering in its impatience. Alfred kept pace with the string of gray-roofed coaches, which from above were dirty round things cluttered with stubby vents. Rising again, he watched how the train shrank away beneath him. Ahead, the mountains were very dark and tall, their pips piercing the level bottoms of the clouds like the peaked cold heads of ancient Druids. Alfred felt by now that he could leave the valley's protection, and he ascended towards the overcast, looking up as he went. The clouds came down to meet him, and he had one last look at the valley below, before he was swallowed up in the mists.

And then it seemed that he was back on the ground. Everything closed tightly in around him. But of course, there was no ground, only the white-gray vapors. He was inside the clouds, and they were very cold. The blades of the heliodrome chopped into the dampness, sending the fog past his face, where it stung with its chill. He took deep breaths of it, and kept climbing.

Just when he doubted he would ever emerge again, he saw the air around him beginning to brighten. Unexpectedly, he was in the clear again, free of the encroaching mist, washed in glorious sunlight.

A wonderland of white lay all about him. Cranking the crank, Alfred paddled above the white blanket, glaring so brightly that he had to avert his eyes in order to see. The air was warmer up here, and with his other hand he undid the top buttons of his coat. He cranked easily, and drifted westward.

Here he was, he thought, all alone in the realm of the eagles. Only a few of the tallest mountains reared their ice-coated peaks upward through the whiteness. No other man had ever seen what he was seeing now. He turned the little whirring gearbox, it sang back to him, and the sturdy blades ate up the air happily. He sang himself a song, with his remaining breath, to celebrate.

The sun was going down into the west when Alfred decided to descend a bit, to look for a break in the clouds. His arm was getting tired, and he remembered the lunch the pitchman had given him, and which he had packed inside his coat.

Finding an opening, through which he could see the landscape below, he looped casually downward through the clear, cooling air, and eased well off his usual pace at the crank. Below, pine forests were darkly spread over the foothills of great granite mountains, and in their center was a sparkling lake.

Alfred lost more altitude quickly, circling. He was soon cruising just above the rippling emerald-green water. He saw a small sandy beach at the far edge, with a stand of towering pines behind it, and, changing direction, he coasted swiftly across toward it.

Approaching the shore, he stopped cranking, and stepped neatly down onto the pebbly bank without tripping. He strolled up the slope to a circle of boulders, and took off the device which had brought him here. Setting it down beside him, he stretched his arms and looked around for a place where he could make himself comfortable in this lovely, isolated spot.

He would camp here tonight, and gather some fallen wood for a fire. He wondered who else might live here, and if anyone had seen him flying over the lake, like some giant, impossible dragonfly. Not that it mattered where he was. As he drifted off to sleep that night, under a canopy of stars, he realized that for the first time in his life he was totally happy.

The next day he took off again, rising into the blue sky, surrounded by mountains like Valkyrie castles.

Many days of traveling followed, days when Alfred flew over hills and valleys, rivers and orchards, forests and canyons, places no ordinary traveler could've ever visited. But Alfred had become extraordinary, flying alone and liking it, borne aloft by his heliodrome.

He followed glittering streams to their sources, chased deer over the shoulders of hills, slept in cool green meadows or under trees whose branches were stirred by vagrant night breezes. He walked over the granite faces of huge unclimbable mountains and stepped off their edges, turning his heliodrome's crank and whop-whopping away into midair. He touched down in the centers of blazing deserts, and took off again when the heat became unendurable. He dipped his toes into inaccessible lakes, and held quiet conversations with mountain goats.

Sometimes when he wanted, he would land and walk, the heliodrome still strapped in place, along winding trails or the edges of roads. People who passed him smiled and waved, apparently unconcerned about the propeller standing motionless atop its shaft, over his head.

His journey was the fulfillment of a dream. By turning the crank, he could rise into the sky whenever he wanted, hovering upward and away, out of sight, quickly and serenely.

And, sometime later, Alfred hush-paddled down from an ocean fog, appearing above a windblown grove of cypresses near a hidden cove of the Pacific. Among the trees was a large white house, built on a hillside, overlooking the view. He circled softly through the trees, his propeller turning, and stepped lightly onto a broad, cool terrace.

Here was a final place to linger before he arrived home. It had been a wondrous journey, and he didn't want it to end. This house seemed to be here especially for him. He approached the double row of glass doors leading inside. They weren't locked. He opened them and stepped through into a gigantic room filled with strange luxuries. Doors opened into other rooms beyond.

Nobody else seemed to be here.

Alfred unstrapped his heliodrome and took it off. He set it down alongside him, then looked around. Satin-upholstered couches and sofas surrounded him, tables laden with books and maps, chandeliers overhead, and elegantly framed paintings on the distant walls. A globe of the world stood in a corner. He finally selected a chair near a piano. A table on the other side held a bowl filled with fruit and nuts, which he sampled, munching. Picking up a book, he turned the pages, looking at pictures of European cities.

He began to feel drowsy, as the sound of the ocean echoed up from below the cliffs, outside the doors, which he'd left open. The room was so peaceful, the cypresses outside so relaxing, that soon he got up, sought out one of the nearby couches, and lay down.

Immediately he was asleep.

He woke to the sound of singing.

Opening his eyes, he sat up.

It was now early evening, and the light from the terrace was fading. The great room now glittered with other light, from the chandeliers, and dozens of smaller lamps on the tables and beside the couches.

A girl, very attractive, wearing a long, flowing garment, sang to herself while she arranged flowers in a vase. She saw him looking at her and turned.

"Hello," she said, smiling.

Alfred blinked. She was indeed lovely.

"Have you been here long?" he asked.

"Oh, a while. You've been sleeping all afternoon."

"I realize." He looked down at himself. "Please excuse me for coming in without being invited – "

She came closer. "You're perfectly welcome. But later tonight, now that you're awake, I'll show you a proper bed where you can sleep."

He stood up and introduced himself.

"And I'm Gloria," she said, taking his hand. Then she glanced behind herself. "What's that?"

His gaze followed hers. "A heliodrome."

Gloria walked over and picked it up. "It certainly doesn't weigh much. What does it do?"

"With that," he told her, moving closer, "I can fly. That's how I came here today. I flew."

She looked again at him, while turning the crank experimentally. "I figured you must have. There are no roads, or even any trails, leading here from further inland. The only way you can get here is by sea, if you have a boat."

"Is that where you came from?"

"A long time ago. I haven't been away from here in years."

Later she led him into a large dining room where someone had laid out supper on a table. He sat down facing the covered dishes. "Do you have servants? I saw no one when I came here earlier."

Gloria sat across from him. "They stay downstairs."

After eating, they shared glasses of wine, and he told Gloria about his journey. The salt-scented breeze on the terrace outside blew cooler, as a full moon rose over the hills to the east, throwing shadows past the arches.

They eventually grew tired of talking, as the night closed in. Soon they were sleep in their separate upstairs rooms.

Alfred stayed a week, tasting the myriad pleasures of Gloria's house. Never once did he see a cook, maid or butler, but the food and drinks appeared, the carpets were clean, the books had been dusted, the tables, the piano, and the globe were polished.

He never solved the mystery of who Gloria was, what her family did for a living, or why this giant house was here.

She accompanied him when he put on the heliodrome once again and walked out onto the sunlit terrace.

He turned to face her, taking her hands in his. "Thank you for a wonderful interlude."

"Thank you for being a gracious guest."

He stepped back from her, and turned the crank, waving with his other hand. As he lifted off, she blew him a kiss.

He rose easily between the trees, above the roof, over the rounded hills beyond. Looking down, he saw the jagged, crescent beach with its white froths of waves. The sea was especially beautiful from up here.

Alfred wanted to get home to Riverport today, and so he ascended even farther, turning inland for a while, to fly in a straighter line.

He passed over Epson, and Creston, and the rail line leading to the Blue River sawmill. He found the woods south of Dunbury, and followed the road from there to the river. He was so glad to see the river again that he almost lost his bearings, before he got back on the right track. Heading downstream just a few feet over the water, he floated serenely around the last few bends towards the sea.

And there, on the bluff, was Riverport. He found Justin Street, and fluttered down in front of a white house with green shutters. His mother came out, followed by his brothers and sisters. Their faces lit up. He was home!

He dined that night on turkey and dressing with all the trimmings, and apple cobbler with ice cream. His father made him welcome, and his brothers Joey and Mark showed him his room, which they'd kept just as he'd left it.

As for the heliodrome, it did not go unnoticed.

His father marveled at the simple effectiveness of the mechanism, as did his older brother Edward, who tried it on, and managed to ascend well out of sight from the back landing, while Alfred and his father watched. He was back in a moment, convinced.

Alfred was certain that such a common-looking thing as his

heliodrome would certainly be in plentiful supply at the general mercantile in town. Edward wanted one, and had ten dollars saved. Father promised Joey and Mark that he'd buy them each one too, for their birthdays. Julie and Jennifer weren't going to let their brothers have anything they couldn't have themselves, and even Mother wasn't one to hold back.

Together, they all rode down to Main Street. The proprietor was fascinated by Alfred's heliodrome. But not only didn't he carry any, he didn't know anyone else in town who possibly could.

None of the stores in Riverport had one. Nor in Letterwich, Bottomley, Cranmouth or even Bedford. In two months, Father made a trip with Alfred and Edward over the mountains to Salem. But no heliodromes were to be found there, either.

Finally, the entire family managed the long and arduous train ride into Portland. But in none of the department stores, even the largest one downtown, could they find a single heliodrome. Nobody even knew what a heliodrome was.

What with everybody taking turns flying with Alfred's heliodrome, it was soon well-worn, and had to be repaired. Years went by, as Alfred and the rest of his family grew older, and nowhere did any of them ever find another heliodrome.

Eventually, with years of rugged use behind it, Alfred's heliodrome came to pieces, and had to be thrown away.

Dynamo

The telephone in the kitchen rang just as John Martin was about to rip another ruined page out of his typewriter. He sat in the closed-off den, hearing it ringing and ringing, unanswered, and began to grit his teeth.

Outside, the Santana was blowing furiously.

He asked himself, where was Alice? She's supposed to answer the telephone when I'm busy, isn't she?

He'd been trying since this morning to write another chapter in his novel, and the damnable frustration he'd felt all afternoon had left him wrung-out and feverish, nerves stretched to breaking. The words simply hadn't come.

The wind hadn't helped either. All day it had blown, a bone-dry blast from the desert, which made the trees beat against the little suburban house and howl in their leaves. And now, in the gathering blue darkness of dusk, it still blew, gusting dreadfully. A panic-stricken branch walloped his window. His nose ached with the dryness, and his skin prickled irritatingly.

The phone kept ringing.

With a mild curse, he finally got up from his workbench and walked over to the door, flinging it open. He hurried through the darkened, dust-smelling house and into the kitchen with one light burning. Skirting a cabinet where he always skinned his knee, he fetched a massive blue spark from an edge of the dinette table with his finger, and it made him wince joltingly, startled. He grabbed the wall phone receiver off its cradle. "Hello!"

Nobody answered. "Hello! Hello!"

The line clicked, and went dead.

As the inane buzzing filled one ear, and the wind tickled at the other, he stood there in mute frustrated fury, wishing he could somehow trace the party who'd just now left him cold. He wanted to wring the fellow's neck.

"Damn!" He put the receiver back on its cradle. He turned in the faint light of the single overhead bulb in the dinette, and found the service porch open, as well as the outside door.

"Alice?" he said, striding out of the kitchen. He found her under the clothesline, wrestling with madly windblown bedsheets and shirts, her arms full of towels and a laundry cart threatening to topple over beside her, in the wind.

"Alice!" he shouted. She turned.

"Why the hell couldn't you answer that phone? You know I'm working!"

"I was working too," she said, "or didn't you notice? I didn't even hear your precious telephone. The wind is ruining my laundry. *Look* at this mess!"

He followed her as she struggled into the house with a hamper loaded full of clothes, and more in her arms. She carried it into the hall, while he went to the kitchen sink for a glass of water to fend off his parched throat.

When she came back, her expression was haggard. "You can't expect me to be everywhere at once, you know. I've got that damned wash to get out, and that wind's blown dust all over this house. I just cleaned yesterday. Now, look at it! Besides, I wanted you to help me with the yardwork today, and where were you? Sitting on your rump in that crazy room of yours!"

"I've got work to do in there!"

She sat down with him at the table, brushing aside her windblown hair with one hand. "Okay, dear," she said. "Did you finish anything today?"

He looked at his hands. "No."

"What?" She sounded furious.

"I couldn't get anything off the ground. It all went stale on me."

"And you were in there all day?!"

"Is it any wonder I'm on edge?" he said. "It's much more nerve-wracking when you can't write, than when you can."

She was silent for a long moment.

"I think you'd better get a job," she said.

He appeared stunned, as though she had slapped him. He stared at her. "What do you mean?" he said.

"Exactly what I said. How much money have we got left? Twenty dollars in the checking account? And with more bills due at the end of the month?" She drilled him with her eyes, piercing. "How much money did you make last year?"

"You know! I sold three stories, and a novel, last year. I made…"

"You made nine hundred dollars."

"That's right. Nine hundred dollars, writing. And solely from writing, mind you!"

He said this last thing as though he felt intense pride in his achievement. To make nearly a thousand dollars from writing alone was a dream come true for John Martin, something he'd wanted to do all his life. He was fired from his fifteenth regular job over a year ago, and had vowed never to work for wages again. And last year he'd worked every day in the den, and made nine hundred dollars.

But for some reason unfathomable to him, Alice didn't see it as such an achievement now. And only a few weeks ago, she'd celebrated with him as the check for the third story came in, a check for seventy-five dollars, coming just in time to pay the month's bills.

But now, she scowled at him.

"I'm tired of being so broke all the time," she said. "I'm tired of having to take out that damn laundry all the time. I want a new dryer, like everyone else has.

"And, I'm tired of having to live in this dump of a house, stuck out here in the boondocks. But it's all we can afford, because my father left it to me in his will, and you don't have enough money to buy a better one! I'm tired, John, just plain tired!"

He kept looking at her, at the new hardness in her face, the new meanness he saw in her eyes for the first time. He couldn't believe what he heard.

"But I wanted to make it work my way, don't you see? I've got to stick it out, and finish this novel, and sell it to New York, and make it my way."

"That stinking novel," she muttered.

"You haven't even read it!"

"I told you before," she said, "I don't want to read anything you write until you've sold it."

"Then, why haven't you read my stories, or my other novel?"

"Because you stooped to write for that cheap men's publisher, to make some quick money, and that kind of sex trash turns my stomach."

He bowed his head. "I try and I try, and you never even thank me..."

"Now don't get maudlin."

He felt his whole world coming to pieces, all of a sudden. He felt suddenly betrayed, lost, abandoned by this woman, loved and now scorned, held once and now tossed aside by this spiteful, selfish creature who felt concern only for automatic dryers, houses and herself.

He got up from the table.

"I will not get a job," he said defiantly, not looking at her. "I'll never work for those bastards who hire people and force them to slave themselves to death for a profit, ever again. Do you hear?" He stalked into his den.

Alice got up and followed him. She came to the doorway and stood in it. Seeing her there, he turned and faced her. "And if you want money that bad," he grated, "then mortgage this damn house for it. If you want a goddamn dryer, or a fur coat, or a stinking Jaguar, go ask your almighty father!"

"Why, you pompous, self-righteous idiot!" she said, standing her ground. "You think you're better than anyone else? You think you're some kind of genius or something?"

He paced across the den, his rubber shoe soles buffing the carpet. He came to his writing table, and touched the swingaway lamp. A sizeable spark leaped at his fingertip. "God damn!" he howled.

"Oh, you poor thing," she said.

He spun on his heel. "Get out of here! Close that door and go away somewhere. I don't want to look at you."

"I will not," she replied. "It's my house, and I'll go wherever I want in it! If you won't consider getting a job, like any real man would, if you just want to hide in this room of yours all day like a little baby, I'll just stand here for as long as I please, and tell you what a big stupid fool you really are!"

He turned, and got his wallet. He cursed under his breath, at his wife and her mouth full of sudden acidic hatreds. He eyed her balefully.

And as he touched his desk, he got another brilliant blue spark that sent him jumping. He got yet another as he touched the doorknob, elbowing past his wife.

"I'm leaving. I'll be back late," he muttered, striding down the hall. He got his coat from the closet, torturing himself once again with the static electricity he'd built up during his walk from the den, as he touched the doorknob.

"Go ahead and go," said Alice. Her dress clung stickily to her legs with electricity, and it made a nasty crackle when she kept pulling it away from herself. "Where are you going? Away forever?"

"Don't wait up for me," he mumbled.

"You gonna be gone that long, eh?"

"I...I'm gonna go buy some booze. Some beer, maybe, and a fifth. There's nothing in this house to drink!"

"Hah!" She laughed. "You're too cheap to even go to a bar for a drink. You'd rather go to a goddamn supermarket!"

"I live here too, you know," he half-whined.

Outside, the Santana kept up its frenzy. They could both hear it, as it screamed through the naked branches of trees, battered at closed windows and garage doors, and tried its best to peel the shingles off the roof. It was obviously a royal-blue night outside, scrubbed sparkling by the wind but still unbearable for all its beauty, not fit to live in.

"Well," she said, "it's too bad you're giving up your diet. You weren't going to touch a drop until you'd lost that gut around your middle. I'm sorry for you." She took a breath. "And, if that's the way it's going to be, you might as well pick me up a pack of cigarettes, too. Or maybe a whole carton. I feel like letting myself go."

"All *right*," he said. He grasped the knob of the front door, recoiling at the newest shock. "*Gaaaah!*"

"That's static electricity," she said, as if she were explaining it to a one-year-old. "It's caused by the wind. When the wind blows, and you wear rubber shoes, you idiot, and you go and touch anything metal, whammie! And only a *child* like you could complain about it."

He opened the front door. Standing there, he let the torrents of wind engulf him for a moment. And then he stepped out, closing the door behind him. He could just barely hear Alice going away from the door, into another part of the house, probably the living room.

And then he went to the garage, threw up the heavy door so that it slammed into the beam overhead, and got into his car. It was a battered old Ford, badly in need of repairs, and the sight of it rebuked him. Maybe she was right! Maybe he should realize that it was a losing battle, this business of trying to be creative and free, and throw in the towel. Maybe he wasn't cut out to be a writer, no matter how much he loved writing, and dreamed about making it pay off.

But then he shook his head. No, damn it! He banged his fist against the steering wheel. He'd never simply give up, never! He had too much pride to do that, too much faith in himself. After all, he'd tried being a writer for sixteen years now, and that was too much time to just throw away.

Besides, it would brand him as a failure for the rest of his life, to give up like that. Alice would probably love him for a while, working steady again, but eventually she'd grow to hate him. He'd be impossible to live with, annoyed by his job, dismayed by his life, disgusted with himself.

The wind kept blowing, sending hordes of dead leaves into the garage around his car. Instead of starting the motor, John sat in the dark, listening to the Santana. It came out of the northeast like a funnel, a whirlwind, and blew due southwest toward the sea, screaming.

What was happening? he asked himself. Why had he and Alice blown up at each other tonight? Did she really want him to quit his writing? Did he really resent her wanting to have nicer things, and maybe life a bit easier? They both had the same desires, in the final analysis. They both wanted happiness and comfort, success and peace of mind.

So why were they fighting?

And why were they so all-fired ready to give up all of their best-laid plans for dieting and trying to quit cigarettes? What was this insanity? This suicidal mania? The wind beat and beat at John Martin's ears.

Realization flooded into him.

Slowly, deliberately, he got back out of his car. He closed the garage door, and went back to the house. Alice heard him come in through the front door, and heard it shut behind him. He stepped quietly into the living room.

She looked at him. "Well, what is it now?"

He came over to her, and sat beside her on the davenport. And before he reached for her, he got out his car keys and grounded himself on a nearby lamp, making the spark with the tip of the metal key.

"Do you know why we're at each other's throats tonight?" he said, taking her hands in his.

"...No, I really don't."

"It isn't you, is it? You don't really hate me."

She shook her head, tears beginning at the corners of her eyes. "And you don't hate me, either," she said. "So, what could it be, darling, that makes us do this?"

"The Santana. That's what. This awful wind." He put an arm around her, pulling her close. They sat together, looking out the living room picture window at the wind-mad landscape. Under a violet sky studded with stars, maddened trees lashed one another with their bony branches, the last of their leaves pulled off an hour ago.

"It's like a dynamo," he continued. "And we've been living inside it for days now, using each other for atom-smashers. We've been building up charges, each of us, until we couldn't help hurting one another with the sparks. Think about it. Just like those trees out there, the wind's been making us beat each other senseless!"

And, sitting there, Alice knew he was right, knew she was through hurting and being hurt by him. She loved him. With his arm still around her shoulder, she twisted around in order to kiss him.

The sparks were still there...but they felt more like fireworks now.

Platform in the Sky

I sensed it before I was fully awake. The dusk I had fallen asleep waiting for, without knowing it, had finally come. And tonight it was somehow different.

All day today, I remembered, the city had lay under a heavy pall of gray smog, turning the sky dead white, and the sun pale orange. For weeks it had been like this, becoming worse as summer refused to yield its grip, stubbornly keeping autumn at bay.

Now, like a child who knew that Christmas was here, I roused myself out of my chair, in the darkened ground-floor apartment. I knew that tonight my years of loneliness, of not being loved, would end. I felt a disturbing pain in my side as I got to my feet, a sharp, sudden jolt of agony. But it vanished almost at once.

I'd had a near-miss today, as I'd been on my way home a few hours earlier, from my workshop at the art institute.

If I closed my eyes now I could still see the onrushing van as it barreled around the far corner and tore toward me through the crowded intersection. I saw the amber, smog-filtered sunshine glittering on its diamond-bright chrome...

It had been a miracle, I knew.

But I clearly recalled walking the rest of the way to the bus stop on rubbery legs, then watching the bus pull away without me, oddly, as if the weary, or perhaps merely distracted driver hadn't seen me standing there. After that, I had walked the three-odd miles home on my own, through dingy, grubby, familiar neighborhoods, down endless side streets lined with dark, dreary shops, along cracked sidewalks thronging with tired, irritated pedestrians like me.

But now, in this magical moment, in the purple dusk, my memories of the day no longer seemed real or important. They were more like a dream that had been interrupted when I awoke, something now gone as swiftly as mist.

My easel stood where I'd left it, the sheet of artboard on which I'd been doing another magazine illustration leaning there in front of me like an old friend, its surface invisible now, with the closed drapes glowing dimly behind it. Maybe I would complete the acrylic tomorrow, then take it down to the girlie publisher to collect my fifty-dollar check. One earned one's living where one could get it.

But for now I had more exciting adventures in mind. There was no one here, at the moment, to keep me from going outside to see if the wondrous glow seeping into the room really meant that the lavender color of the dusk had *changed...*

I moved breathlessly toward the street-side door, and opened it. Then, I stepped out onto the narrow concrete pavement by the building's decorative rock garden...into the wind.

The wind – !

It whistled out of the north, clear and cold, scrubbing the sky clean.

Above the nearby buildings that cluttered the horizon, a single white cloud still lingered in a region of pale pastel blueness far away to the west, impossibly distant. It seemed to hover in an entirely alien sky, perhaps above some exotic, remote mountain kingdom watched over by a shimmering alabaster castle on a soaring summit...

The cloud, shaped like a silver starship, hypnotized me as I stared at it. A sudden desire gripped me, to escape from this neighborhood, to abandon my life, and the art institute, and the unfinished painting, and all of my other half-done projects and half-baked ambitions, and never return.

I felt an overwhelming conviction that I could do things this evening, which I had never tried before.

I wanted to travel to that castle near the cloud, where a beautiful princess probably waited, imprisoned, guarded by enchanted, unconquerable dragons.

I shut my door and came down over the rocks toward the street, arriving on the nearly invisible sidewalk in the gathering evening. I turned eastward, putting the dreamlike image of the western sky behind me so I wouldn't see it.

I moved casually along through the blasts of wind, jamming my hands down into the pockets of my wrinkled work pants. I tried to empty my mind of all thoughts, simply hoping to enjoy the remarkable excitement I could feel as I gazed up at the blues, purples and violets which shimmered now off every wind-whipped tree and wind-washed building.

The street was a river alongside me, an Amazon flowing from forever past into forever future, a deep clear waterway that might lead into worlds of which I had never, until tonight, been the least bit aware.

Soon I had arrived at a cross street. Someone else was also out here in the wind. Which seemed strange because all the rest of the world had been entirely empty.

As the rushing air roared in my ears, as though it wanted to surge through into my mind, I saw the ghostly feminine figure standing only a few feet from me. She was holding her thin, pale arms out at both sides of herself like wings, slightly lifted, so that her gossamer dress flowed forward from her, carried on the wind.

I knew she was beautiful, even while the fabric obscured her face. Finally she lowered her arms and moved a bit nearer, reaching up to pull her long silver hair away from her eyes.

"Hi," she said brightly.

"Hello." My voice sounded as unfamiliar as everything else about this strange dusk. "What were you doing, trying to fly?"

She laughed, a thrilling ripple of sound in the enveloping gusts. "I guess I was," she admitted. "In this marvelous wind, I almost feel like I could."

As I faced her, I failed to recognize her. "Are you from around here?" I asked.

She shook her head. "I used to live here, so I come back to visit the old street every once in a while, to see how things have changed." We started to walk southward together, down an empty sidewalk past the blank walls of warehouses and the dusty glass fronts of dilapidated industrial shops. "The smog's been terrible," she said. "I'm not used to it anymore. Where I've been living lately, out in the desert, there's almost never any haze at all. Today, here in town, I couldn't get a deep breath. Then tonight, the wind came. If it weren't for this wind, I think I would've died."

Soon we stood at another corner, under an awesome expanse of sky, still faintly blue. The street in front of us was eerily unoccupied. No traffic seemed to be moving anywhere tonight, I realized. At a larger avenue, one block away to the darkening east, a traffic light changed its Christmas colors again and again, though nobody was around to pay any attention.

Why, I wondered suddenly, did the whole city seem so vacant, this early in the evening?

As the silver-haired girl and I looked out across the flat, bare pavement of the desert-like intersection, in the slate-gray half-light, the wind pulled and tugged at both of us, making her long hair stream ahead of her like a flag. "Feel that!" she exulted. "God, I honestly think I could fly!"

I mimicked her ridiculous seagull pose. The wind bellowed.

Then she put her arms down again and pointed. "See that tall, flat-topped building way over there, about six blocks away?"

I nodded. Its clear glass sides reflected an aquamarine and purple glow.

"Have you ever wanted to sneak up onto the roof of a building," she asked, "just so you could go out to the very edge and look down?"

I peered sideways at her. "Uh-huh," I said. "I used to do that a lot, when I was a kid."

She grinned. "Did you ever get caught?"

"A few times. Once, a particularly nasty super who nabbed me when I was on my way up the last flight of stairs threatened to call the police and have me sent to reform school."

"Well," the girl said, still looking at the building, "let's go up there now."

"But how?" I asked. "That could take hours. The light'll be gone by the time we get there."

"Maybe not," she said.

Then she held her arms back up.

As I watched, raising my own hands again, the girl began to move across the street, drifting away. The wind blew stronger than ever. I kept my eyes on her, not wanting to break the spell of the fantastic lifting sensation the wind was giving to my arms. I glanced below the hem of her long dress, and a startled chill flashed through me.

Her bare feet, extending downward, hung in plain sight below the gossamer fabric, but they weren't touching the pavement. The toes, small and pale, pointed delicately toward the asphalt, drifting silently over it.

Like an angel, the girl floated across the intersection, as light as a soap bubble. While I stared with numb shock at this blatant impossibility, the wind sang like a chorus of a thousand voices in my ears. It streamed by me, the street also sliding past, underneath me.

The girl and I, I discovered, were staying about the same distance apart, though I could clearly see that she was moving faster all the time, and rising higher into the air. She was already almost to the far curb, floating high enough now to clear the corner of a parking lot.

She looked back at me while she flew.

"Do you feel it?" she asked joyously. "Do you feel the wind lifting you up?"

I felt it, my heart hammering in my chest.

Then I looked down.

The street was far below me.

Ahead, the girl folded her arms inward against her sides. The wind pushed her forward, and she shot away like a bullet, dwindling into the sky.

"Wait for me!" I called, like a child.

As I tucked in my own arms, the wind abruptly gripped me with unexpected force.

I accelerated breathlessly.

Together, the girl and I rose toward the distant building. Farther and farther below me, the neighborhood of flat-roofed commercial buildings formed an abstract pattern of thrilling complexity from this angle.

I trembled as I became aware that I was looking down at all of this through sixty, seventy, eighty feet of nothingness, which meant that there was no way I should be up here at all, so far above the ground, suspended, hovering, floating.

My heart thundered with the exultant excitement of it.

We both came to the roof of the high-rise at about the same time. Laughing, the girl reached back and took hold of my hand as she cleared the brink at the top of the building's wall and stepped lightly down onto the gritty roofing beyond.

She pulled me after her, and the two of us fell onto our backs, looking up just in time to see the first really bright stars blinking into view high overhead, in the opalescent, jewel-clear sky.

"Here we are!" she said, catching her breath.

"We did it, didn't we!" I said.

"You and I," she said.

"Together!"

All at once she rolled over onto me, straddling me as I still lay on my back. Her shimmering hair draped down onto my chest while she leaned forward to touch me.

Then, we were kissing. I pulled her down against me, feeling her warmth, her solidity, the perfect firmness of her body, her breasts pushing into my chest through the gauzy clothing, her breath blowing over my cheek as her lips moved across mine, blending, mingling, seeking and accepting.

Here we were, I thought, repeating her words to myself. She was the first girl I'd kissed since I'd left my home a thousand miles away, and what seemed like a thousand years ago, and had moved to this alien, hostile city.

I couldn't seem to help myself now, any more than I'd been able to keep the wind from bringing me up here, along with this just-now stranger, this girl, this female, who had changed quite suddenly to become my companion, my friend, my lover.

The wind still blew, stronger here than it had on the streets so far below, whipping and buffeting and pulling at the two of us in its haste to take us further into the night.

I could feel our hearts beating in the same rhythm.

An amazing, wonderful realization flashed over me. She wanted me as much as I wanted her! We had an equal desire for each other, here in the enchanted night, on this low-walled island in the endless sky. We were like two castaways on a faraway beach, sharing each other because there was nobody else in the world to know, or to forbid.

Nor did either of us want our pleasure to end merely with kissing.

Her hands sought me with an urgent desperation, while her lips remained sealed to mine. She struggled to find me in the dark, and then she did. Having moved down her body, my hands now grasped her hips, two rounded pillows of flesh, which seemed to fit my caressing fingers with startling exactness.

I didn't want to wait a second longer for the culmination.

Nor did she.

The gossamer parted.

Soon I felt her all around me. I embarked on a journey into her, exploring her, feeling her absorb me. Beyond her head, through strands of hair that separated like lace curtains, I still saw the stars twinkling in the nighttime sky.

The stars seemed to be laughing.

Afterward, both the girl and I were so filled with love that it was as if we shone with an inner light like furnaces in the darkness. We held hands as I led her to the far edge of the roof and simply stepped away into space. We drifted off eighteen floors above the hard pavement and the factory roofs below. Like two meteorites, we ascended into crystal-clear space, and soared over the city, which shrank to a patchwork of lights below. I caught up with her as she leveled off, and moved closer alongside her.

"Is this real?" I asked through the rush of wind.

"It must be. I can see you just as clearly as anything," she said, "and since I'm up here, then you must be up here too."

She glanced across at me. "Can you see me?"

"Sure." I took a breath. "That means...we're really flying!"

As the stars spread across the sky, we circled over the vast, sprawling city.

"I wasn't being completely honest, earlier," she said, "when I told you that I sometimes liked to come in from the desert, just to visit my old neighborhood."

"What do you mean?" I asked, although I already knew the answer.

She didn't say any more for a few minutes, and at last she went on. "What really happened today, was that my folks had to bring me into the city, in an ambulance, which took me to the hospital."

I peered across at her.

"I had German measles when I was very young," she explained,

99

"and the doctors say it made my lungs so weak that the smog permanently damaged them. My family had to move to the desert in order to keep me from dying."

"So what happened today?" I asked finally.

"It's funny," she said. "I wasn't really awake when they brought me to the hospital. But when I woke up in my room tonight and saw that the sun had gone down, and saw that, because of this wind, the city outdoors was just like my home in the desert, all of a sudden I could remember everything."

Once more, I saw the onrushing van and the crowd of people, heard them screaming, and remembered how I'd felt. Not angry, actually, though the pain had been intense. More embarrassed, since it seemed like such a silly, stupid thing, to let oneself be run over and killed in an intersection...but then I pushed these thoughts out of my consciousness.

"We're never going home again, are we," I said flatly.

She laughed. "Nope. I don't think so."

"Which way would you like to go?" I asked her.

"West," she replied, nodding toward the distant starship cloud. I turned with her, and we started to fly westward.

"What if there was a secret kingdom under that cloud?" she said, "so far away from here that, where it is, the sun is still shining at high noon?"

"With an alabaster palace on a mountaintop?"

"Uh-huh..." She turned to stare in surprise at me. "But how did you know that?"

"Just before I met you," I said, "back there on the street outside my apartment, I saw the silvery cloud above the other buildings, and I could see the same vision. There's a princess in that castle, locked in a high tower."

"Guarded by fierce, enchanted dragons," the girl said. "She has golden hair, covered by a silver veil, and she wears a long, white, gossamer gown."

"And there's a noble knight who's desperately in love with her," I said. "He wears huge black boots, a red cape, dark bronze armor, and a golden helmet. He keeps a falcon for a pet, and rides a white charger."

"I really am that princess," the girl said, "and right now I'm dreaming about flying with my lover, the valiant knight. But soon I'll wake up, and I'll still be trapped in the castle tower."

"This has all been a dream for me too," I said. "When I wake up, I will find that I am down in the valley town, at the inn where I've spent the night, before I ride to the castle gates to rescue you."

"Yes..." we both said afterward.

The shining cloud was much closer now.

Intruder

Gryhl came back into being exactly four hundred years after he had entered suspension for the eighteenth time in his young life.

He flashed along the circuits of Bank Five, Row 203, Level 1209 of the central memory unit in his hometown, North City Development, his molecules finally reassembling in the fabricator.

A full second later, he stepped from the booth facing Ramp AX23384S of U sector, his old home ramp.

Pausing, Gryhl glanced around at the familiar ramp, taking in any changes which might've taken place during his four hundred years of absence. Comfortingly, nothing spectacular had been done. It was still the same Level he'd known and loved.

To him, of course, the four centuries of suspension had gone by totally unnoticed. He'd entered the booth a moment earlier, as he had done so many times, and had now emerged again. Had he not known beforehand that he was being encoded for another period of stasis, he'd have thought he was in a communication booth, or an intergalactic transporter.

He felt as fit as usual, and by the color of the illumination panels overhead, it appeared that another sunny day had been programmed by the weather office. He would've liked rain himself, and made a mental note to choose that this evening, when he arrived back at his cubicle.

Meanwhile, he intended first to visit the Dome Top, to take advantage of his privilege as a newly-restored stasee to a special place in the line waiting for a look at the actual Terran scenery outside the barrier.

Taking one of the many diagonal lifts from his level, he chose a seat between two lovely young-looking women in transparent pastel sheers and waited as he was whisked the 40-odd miles to the top of North City Development.

Colonel Colodney, specially trained and prepared, a hand-picked winner from among thousands of Time Probe applicants, stepped briskly into the gigantic room accompanied by a small army of assistants, carrying his oxygen and life-support equipment in one hand.

A faint flutter of applause went up among the assembled reporters, cameramen, and commentators on the scene. With a brief answering wave and a smile, Colodney stepped inside a yellow circle which had been painted on the polished metal floor and approached the gleaming capsule, Century I.

It was called that because the aim of the experiment was to send a single time-traveler precisely 100 years into the recent past. Colodney's job, when he got there, would be to collect enough physical clues to prove that his trip had actually been a success. He would bring these objects back with him when he returned.

Century I was a time machine. It was the first of its kind that anybody knew of and it represented the culmination of a top-secret project which had cost billions of taxpayer dollars.

"Are you ready, Colonel?" asked Colodney's direct chief in command, General Alvin Besser.

Colodney nodded.

Steeling himself, he climbed through the small hatch into the metallic spheroid.

The press and the television people were allowed to gather momentarily around the open hatch, to give the viewers at home better glimpses of Colodney, who was obliged to wave a few more times at the cameras, and smile gamely as well.

"Enough of this, gentlemen," the general said.

As the media backed away, the hatch of the capsule was swung shut, and dogged down.

The officer at the controls nearby took over.

"Hello, Century I. This is Base Control. Are you reading me clearly?

"You're coming in five-by-five."

"Countdown to Time Launch proceeding." A red toggle switch was thrown. "Twenty seconds. Nineteen. All systems show green for go. Sixteen – "

An air of suspense gripped the onlookers.

Great hidden dynamos kept up a rhythm they'd maintained for weeks beforehand. They hummed loudly under everyone's feet. Lights flashed on banks of panels behind the group of spectators. Eerie screams echoed from wall to wall around the silvery sphere.

The capsule began to glow.

"Ten, nine, eight – "

"Captain..." came Colodney's voice.

"What is it?" said the general into a microphone.

"Five...four...three..."

"I think I'm detecting a malfunction – "

"Zero!"

Century I disappeared.

The yellow circle was suddenly empty. The roar of the machines automatically subsided. All contact had now ceased, since the capsule no longer existed in the present.

General Besser glanced at the man who'd been doing the countdown.

"What did he say, major?"

The other man shook his head. "I don't know, sir. I was busy counting."

Wow, thought Colodney. What a boner. What a goof-up.

The last time he'd looked, his dial had read 2025, a hundred years in the past.

But then the figures had started rolling precipitously forward.

By 'Twelve' on the countdown, they were reading 2125, the present date where Colodney was starting from. By the time the man outside had gotten to 'Two' the numbers had gone past 3125. They continued adding up, reaching half a million, then one and a half million, blending at last into a blur.

He was frankly scared.

"General, I'm scared," he said into his communicator. But it did no good. His capsule seemed to be flashing forward into the future. The general and everybody else were probably millions of years away by now, somewhere behind him in the unrecoverable past.

On his return from the Dome Top, Gryhl stepped out of the crowded lift onto his home level, and headed for his cubicle, a short way further along the ramp. The illumination panels were darkening into a golden sunset over his head by the time he arrived at his solid-looking entrance plate. Stepping up, he walked directly through it.

Because he knew that the sensing devices inside the plate would recognize his unique genetic structure, Gryhl didn't need to worry about bruising himself against an impassable obstacle. Instead, the plate's atomic structure changed into a gas long enough for him to pass through it, then changed back into a metallic solid again.

Inside, his old home cubicle hadn't changed a bit. The floorfield under his feet felt soft and springy, though its color and texture were still only a neutral foggy gray. The ceiling showed the same sunset color as it had out on the ramp.

Walking around the four walls, Gryhl touched each one with a finger.

"Green," he told one. "Red," he said to another. "Dark, wine-colored. Royal blue. And you, maybe a waterfall in a sunlit mountain valley, mid-afternoon, with naked girls in the foreground, dancing in a meadow."

The walls changed to the appropriate colors. The one he'd told to show a waterfall disappeared, becoming a window opening onto a three-dimensional scene which opened out to the horizon. Just beyond the perfectly transparent surface, a troop of somewhat hefty, mother-naked nymphs cavorted over a level expanse of sunlit grass.

"And you," he said to the floor, "be a shallow stream of water flowing over smooth, soft sand."

Splashing his tired feet happily in the water, he sat back to watch the nymphs. A net of invisible fields buoyed his body up as he folded his arms behind his head and crossed his feet.

The view at the Dome Top had been a huge disappointment. The air pollution had thickened considerably. Mighty storms of brown and red mists raged at 40 miles altitude. The sun was no longer visible. He could see rows of other domes, each one scores of miles across, poking up through the cloud layers. Even the nearest cities were only dim outlines through the windblown streamers of murk.

He vastly preferred the view he had now, through the wall he was facing, in his cubicle.

He didn't notice the chromium-colored globe materializing silently in the corner behind him.

The dials and display gauges of Colonel Colodney's machine steadied and stopped. The whole apparatus gave one gentle thump and was still. Without looking again at the time indicator, probably because he was afraid to, he undogged the hatch of his capsule and pushed it open.

A glowing panel of brilliant royal blue, next to another one of deep wine-red, greeted him. They looked like they were velvet-covered, under a magenta-and-orange sunset sky. By its color, Colodney judged he was facing the southwest.

Then he noticed the man. Wearing nothing but vibrantly multicolored tights from neck to ankle, he floated in mid-air only a few feet away from the capsule. He was facing off to the left, looking at something Colodney couldn't himself see. He appeared to be stretched out in a comfortable reclining position, but he was reclining on absolutely nothing.

Colodney briefly weighed the possibilities. He was insane. No. He was hallucinating out of fear. Possibly. This was all a bad dream. He pinched himself. No. He hurt. He was in the future, not in the past.

That had to be it. His malfunction. Or something else. His militarily-trained reasoning reached quick conclusions. It was possible, wasn't it, for the machine to slam up against something the scientists had all theorized about at length with him during briefing, the barrier of history? They had put forth the theory and discarded it as being too far-fetched, that the past may very well be guarded by a vaultlike invisible wall, unchangeable and unenterable.

Could they have been right after all? Colodney decided that it was so, that he had indeed bounced off some impenetrable barrier in time and ricocheted into the future.

But how far into the future? What kind of place was this? He opened the hatch the rest of the way. The air, fresh and crisp, was eminently breathable. It smelled like mid-spring in a forest.

A waterfall was visible on the other side of the floating man. But the sight bothered Colodney. He definitely saw mountains and forests in the distance, a meadow, a glittering stream, a line of naked dancing maidens, and a filmy but magnificent waterfall in the distance.

But the sky outside that window showed midday light, not the sunset sky which was just as real overhead. Colodney did some additional thinking. What he saw above, he assured himself, must be a sheltering translucent roof which filtered the noonday sunlight to sunset intensity, while changing the colors in some way. That it was high noon outdoors was obvious, from looking through the wall.

This was some kind of futuristic mountain cabin, he concluded, and he, by a freak coincidence, had materialized in his capsule inside the cabin.

He began to climb noisily out of the hatch.

Hearing this, the man in the kaleidoscopic tights stepped abruptly to his feet, by simply lowering his legs to the floor and rebounding to a standing position.

Turning, he stared unbelievingly at Colodney's capsule. And also at its occupant, who at the moment was straining to remove his other leg from inside, while disconnecting the last of his life-support gear.

"Ahh..." said Colodney over his shoulder. "Hello."

Who are you? came a thought in Colodney's brain. Colodney stared back at the stranger. Telepathy?

What are you doing in my cubicle?

"I – " Colodney fumbled, feeling very embarrassed, "ahh, I-I made an error..."

Where did you come from? What is that machine?

"Are you...reading my mind?" Colodney stammered. "How come you can still speak English?"

I do not know what an English is. I speak what I speak.

"Don't you...speak with your mouth?"

Only to my machines. They do not have minds.

Colodney didn't know what to do with himself. He twiddled his fingers, staring down at his hands. The other man in the room waited.

"Yes," said Colodney at last. "Well, ahh...yes, I, ahh – "

Your thoughts are very confused.

"You could say that again," he said, mostly to himself. "I want to ask you some questions. What is your...name?"

The numerals and digits that came back flooded into Colodney's consciousness like ball bearings tumbling down a washboard.

"Oh." He shook his head to try and clear it. "What year is this?"

Another scramble of numerical noise.

What's it to you, anyway? the man thought pugnaciously. Nobody asked you to barge into my private cubicle, disturbing my relaxation.

"I'm sorry," Colodney said. "Only, it's very important that I know something else. I've come a long way in my machine, and I guess from your point of view you could say that I'm from a long time ago in your past. I only want to know how far in your past."

What is that sphere anyway? thought the man in the kaleidoscope-suit. A very small spaceship? A teleportation device?

Colodney puffed himself up proudly. "It's a time machine. A means for traveling backward or forward in time." His pride quickly deflated as he added, "at least we thought it would go backward. I guess that's impossible, though." He glanced behind himself in dismay at the metal sphere. "Which means I'm probably stuck here.

"You see," he went on, facing forward again, "our government built this single capsule, spending billions of dollars on the vast arrangement of machinery which was necessary to power it. I was the man they finally selected to be the pilot. We intended to shoot exactly a hundred years into the past. But instead something apparently prevented this, and so now here I am in your time...in my future."

Why do you say you are not in your future?

"Because of what I can see. This is certainly a splendidly-equipped mountain cabin you have here." He looked it over with the air of a prospective homebuyer evaluating a piece of real estate. "Strange glowing walls, no furniture, the way you were reclining in mid-air when I first saw you, the odd ceiling..." He whistled. "This certainly isn't any twenty-first-century shack."

It isn't a mountain cabin either, thought the stranger, tossing in a derogatory thought concerning Colodney's poor perception and low intelligence.

The mountains eroded away long ago. Besides, with all the cities now, we don't have room for mountains, oceans, or even deserts. We are standing in a cubicle deep inside a stupendous dome, facing a wall which is capable of flawlessly projecting any scene I desire so that it becomes more real than any actual window. The ceiling is a similar panel, programmed by the weather office to display whatever sky colors are appropriate for the time of day or night.

My food is synthetic, and more delectable than anything you could imagine, my body's every need is amply served by the machines in these walls. I am many, many centuries old and have no great disillusionments or longings, goals or fears, projects or obligations.

I am a comfortable creature, or was anyway, until you showed up and plopped down your overgrown ball-bearing directly between me and my transplate, Colodney.

"See?" Ignoring the other, Colodney almost danced a jig. "I knew this was the future! Teleportation! Telepathy! Cubicles in gigantic cities which cover the Earth! Every personal desire provided for by machines! I knew it! I knew it! I've bounced off the barrier which kept me from traveling into the past, and have landed here in the future!"

He stared at the man in the tights. "Can you remember the United States?"

What is a United States?

"America! The United States of America! It is, er, was, a powerful democracy in the year 2125, in North America. Far, far in your past! Right?"

I never heard of it. And I have had far more than enough time to scan all the historical and geographical records which are kept in our great central library. Our archaeologists have had centuries in which to excavate every square inch of this planet's surface in search of relics, and none have been found. There is no United States of America on our records.

"Are...are you certain?" said Colodney.

Yes. And furthermore, I refuse to accept your insane suggestion that you might've come here in a time machine. Whatever that sphere behind you might be, it has obviously been electroported here under false pretenses. I used to work as a theoretical physicist. I did research into the possibilities of warping the matrix of the time continuum. I discovered and published more data on the subject than any of my colleagues, and I can assure you beyond a doubt that time travel has always been impossible.

"But – " Colodney faltered, glancing back again at his machine. "But – !"

He sensed his logic collapsing around him.

The professors in his own time had told him one other thing about establishing a reference-point for time travel. The state of scientific research was as sure a yardstick for determining the era of time one might have arrived in, as carbon dating.

He swung away from the man in the tights and leaned, heart pounding, into his capsule to take the first look since his arrival here at the time indicator.

It read 987,046,055 B.C.

Memory

She hit her head on the brass dog.

She had known it was there, because she lived just up the street. But she hadn't seen it. She had been chasing after the others, the light-frocked summer girls, the eagle-eyed, tennis-shoed gazelle boys. Then her foot had slipped in the wet grass of the Fredericks' front lawn, and her head had fallen hard against the gleaming metal of the brass dog.

And she had passed out.

How long ago had that been? Two hours? Three hours? Maybe even a day. One whole day gone from summer!

Summer, 1910.

She remembered the dog sitting there in the grass, in the shadows of the Fredericks' two-century-old elm tree, on a fine residential street of Santa Vera. She could see it so clearly! The metal statue of the dog had always fascinated her. It reposed in the flickering shadows, its head regally raised, as if it was supervising the neighborhood children at their games. It resembled some ancient haughty monarch, far older than anything else in sight. She thought to herself how old that brass dog seemed. Eternal, almost. As though it was part of the landscape, having risen out of the ground. Everything else was temporary. That dog, sphinxlike, had seen the town, the streets, the trees and the houses rise up around it as it watched with its sightless metal eyes. And there it rested, all power and glory, all so solid...

She could feel her childlike senses returning.

She was lying on her back, in a bed. The sheets caressed her with smooth softness, feeling much softer than usual. She felt the sensation of floating...

She fought to remember more.

Had the others seen her fall? They had been running so fast, especially the boys, heading for Forest Park and the glen where the creek ran cool-clear in the shade. They'd been going off to a special place that two of the boys, John and Dennis, knew about, where you could hide and play and never be discovered by the adults.

Had they seen what happened to her? Did they know?

They were probably there right now, ringing her bed, anxiously awaiting her recovery. She tried to see their faces. The dark-haired, strong face of John and the plain, flat-browed face of Dennis, shorter and stockier. The freckled face of Carol and the ruddier face of Esther, with dark liquid eyes. Yes, she told herself assuredly, they were all waiting to see her wake up, all waiting, worried that she might be injured...

A red curtain of pain blotted out their images. A vast hot anvil began to throb, pounding, in the very center of her brain. She struggled, twisting, fighting the agony of the concussion. A flood of nausea welled up, and subsided like a tide.

What time was it? She yearned to know. What day, what hour? Between her consciousness and reality, the screen of metallic and fiery pain arose, shutting off all clocks, calendars, and open bedroom windows. Were her eyes closed or open? She couldn't tell. Were there flickering summer leaves at the window? Was the pale ivory clock sitting on her bedstand, its familiar face like an old friend, like her other friends, waiting for her to wake up and say she felt better? She didn't know.

A feeling of loneliness flooded through her, like a surge of icewater, a frigid gust of air on the side of her face. She felt terribly isolated, cut-off, removed from that summer day. Abruptly, Forest Park was a billion miles away, impossible to reach ever again. She almost cried.

And then, through the continual pulsing of the pain, the repeated pounding of that fiery anvil in her skull, the loneliness congealed, coalesced into an entity. It became dark and real, hideous in its appearance, malevolent. It was old.

She could tell that at once. She felt it.

Whatever faced her, in this private world of her mind, with its sealing-off walls of torment, was horribly old.

And then a second realization frightened her. This shadowy ogre knew her. It recognized her, and looked straight at her.

She remembered her grandfather.

He was sitting on the side of her bed, in her bedroom, in the depth of a winter when frost etched its patterns on the glass of the closed window. The room was filled with warmth, and she was sick with an earlier fever that had her mind reeling with a temperature and also had the rest of the household worried about her, occupied with trying to make her comfortable.

She recalled, she had been arguing with her grandfather.

"How do you know how I feel, Grandpa?" she said, sighing. "Were you ever sick, the way I'm sick now? Were you?"

"Of course." He patted her through the quilts and comforters. "I was a kid once myself. I got sick just like you, and I felt miserable."

"You couldn't have," she remembered saying.

Her grandfather, with skin like leather and bones that you could actually hear creaking when he sat down in the one chair he liked in the living room, was incredibly old. He had venerable old coats and hats, walking-sticks and pipes, that contained a mustiness which none of the family's other possessions held. His books, on a special shelf of the library, had peeling covers or genuine stitched-leather bindings that even her father said weren't being made anywhere anymore, in these modern times.

"Yes indeed," Grandfather retorted, sitting on the bed. She could recall every silver-gray hair that swept past his temples and around his ears as he spoke, could see the faint blueness of his eyes and his gnarled, spotty hand, which held a smoldering, smoke-curling pipe. "I used to live out on the prairie, on a farm, when I was a child. My family moved out there long before there was anything but wilderness. We lived in a house with two rooms, one for living and the other for sleeping. When any of us got sick with a fever, we had to bed down in the sleeping room. And my mother would put on a pot to boil, and cover us up with blankets and quilts and comforters, and would bring hot-water bottles for our feet. And of course, if the fever lingered, my father dragged one of the beds out to the fireplace, and whoever was sick could be right in the center of the family while they got well. But all of that ended when the railroad came through, and we sold the farm to buy a better house in town..."

He lapsed into musing, with his pipe between his teeth and him puffing on it, so that it made a wheezing sound.

"I don't believe you," she remembered saying.

He looked at her out of the corners of his eyes. "Why? Why shouldn't you believe your old grandpa?"

"Because you're so old. You're older than Father. You're older than any of my aunts and uncles. You're even older than Grandma. How could you ever be just a little boy?"

He smiled. "Why are you just a little girl?"

She hadn't understood.

"I don't believe you were ever young," she said through her fever. "You've always been the same...always. You were never like me. You were never young..."

But then the pain was there again, screaming, glaring, intruding upon her remembrances, shattering the visions. Grandfather fell away down a well, gone, turning over and over as he disappeared. She wanted to call after him, but her voice was no longer there. She was alone in a universe of pain.

The pain lidded over her existence like a cloud. But what a cloud it was! Brilliant colors welled in and out of the grayness. Shards of light flashed into the base of her skull and the backs of her eyes, like glass splinters, slicing into her consciousness with fierce torturing.

As it ebbed away, the pain was again replaced by the cold breeze, the brief sensation of aloneness and far isolation, and the black ogre with the familiar visage. Old, she thought. Young and old together...incompatible.

What time was it? Where was the clock?

And where was she? Suddenly, the bed in which she lay felt strangely alien, not her own bed but somebody else's. She seemed to see, to feel, to touch, to know!

How old was Grandfather? Nobody had any idea.

She didn't know of many other people who could be older than he.

Except, perhaps, for old Mrs. Ramsbottom.

*

She lived on the corner and liked to sit just inside the screen of her sun porch and watch the people go by, the children on the sidewalk. And now and then she would say things to nobody in particular, in that croaking, froglike, nearly inaudible voice of hers.

Most of the children in the neighborhood feared the old woman, said she was a witch, that she never slept nights but continued to sit inside the concealing density of the screening, with her pale unseen eyes roving here and there over the street, bringing curses upon whoever displeased her.

The children always gave the Ramsbottom porch a wide berth after dark, despite the fact that nobody could tell whether or not there was actually anyone waiting, any sinister human form sitting inside the screens.

Once, the children had gathered to discuss old Mrs. Ramsbottom and her all-seeing eye, sitting around the shiny sleekness of the brass dog in the deep grass of the Fredericks' front lawn.

Esther said that she thought those froglike sounds the old woman uttered unexpectedly were definite signs that she had just hexed somebody, and that anyone who was passing at the time was sure to have nightmares for a week and wake up screaming, or lose something valuable, or develop warts on their tongue, or go deaf in one ear, or have cramps or a fever, or get a spanking from the grownups for something they hadn't done.

Immediately, the kids had taken count of all the times they'd been passing the Ramsbottom porch when there had come one of the old woman's croakings. And sure enough, each time it had occurred, the victim had almost immediately been visited with one form or another of disaster, infirmity, failure, or misfortune.

Then, she herself had told the others about the time when she'd had the fever and Grandpa had argued that he was once young.

"Do you think, maybe," Esther proposed, "that we'll all grow old? Do you think we'll ever get as old as Mr. Hobson who runs the tobacco store, or Mr. Bennett at the soda parlor, or Mr. Chittell the trolley operator, or..." and here she hesitated because the idea was so frightful, "or even old Mrs. Ramsbottom?"

And everyone had agreed.

Nobody could start out young, and ever get to be as hideously old, as terrifying with age, as monstrous and senile and abominable as old Mrs. Ramsbottom.

The pain returned. It seemed to move in cycles.

First came the awareness, the sensation of being isolated and alone. Then the black ogre with the familiar silhouette. And finally the memory, images of summer fleeting and reappearing, the children in the neighborhood, her own family.

Then, finally, there was the pain.

The circle of summer-warm children, sitting in their frocks and knickers on the cool, shady grass around the Fredericks' brass dog, swam on the edge of vanishing.

"Will we ever get old?" a boy named Walter was saying.

"Not me," answered a girl. "I'll never get old. I don't want to be like Mrs. Ramsbottom, or Mr. Chittell, or anybody else who's that old. No, not me. I'm going to stay young forever."

The pain welled back up like lava in a volcano, like the stuff that erupts when one is sick and vomits, like fire in the belching blast furnaces she'd once seen when Father had taken her and her brother into the industrial section of a nearby city, and she'd come home and had nightmares for weeks afterward about falling into pits of red-hot melted steel, unable to stop herself, screaming all the way down.

"I'm going to stay young forever," came the echo of the nameless girl. "Going to stay young forever, stay young forever..."

The girl and the other children were suddenly very far away. They were at the other end of a giant telescope, a crystal tunnel, shrinking into invisibility even as she watched.

"...going to stay young...forever..."

She couldn't even see the brass dog anymore. It dwindled away, down and down, unreachable through the pain.

"...forever...stay young..."

The black outline was there. The summer was gone. The shadow had replaced it. Gone were the cool green leaves overhead, the cool green grass under one's knees and hands, and the warm sunlight.

"...forever..." came the echo, impossibly distant.

The pain came and went, in sickening surges.

And she remembered a bog of clay, a slimy pool, a tarn, that she'd seen in back of the Monarch house around the corner and in the next block, on a morning made special by its horror.

Long, long ago, the adults said, so the town legends had gone, there had been a little girl who lived in the house before the Monarch family had bought it and moved in. And one rainy day she had simply vanished.

They said that she'd failed to come in out of the rain, was looking for something at the rear of the downward-sloping yard, was dressed in only light clothing, and was never seen again. They said that her mother saw her from a back window of the house, where she was searching among the thick clumps of grass, and turned to leave the house and fetch her, and never found her.

They said all this happened fifty years ago.

And that morning, the morning that bloomed up full-blown into memory, like a clear and perfect stereopticon slide, she arrived at the Monarch house with a group of the other kids, to join a great silent crowd of adults in the Monarchs' back yard.

Mr. Monarch had been contemplating a vegetable garden, had found the soil too soft and squishy, fed with water seeping up from underneath, so that one sank swiftly into it unless one was careful. He'd begun digging into the soft clay, in an attempt, so the grownups said afterward, to find the source of the spring, if he could, and had unexpectedly unearthed a thing that sent him gasping into the house, his shovel forgotten.

And there, in the sunlight on that awful morning, she had seen it with the other children.

A human hand.

It was pale-gray, small and slender, and slimy with peat. Its fingernails were blackened from the tannin in the peat, and the flesh sagged in slippery folds from the bones. But it could nevertheless be recognized and identified. It was the hand and arm of a young girl who had been buried for all these decades in the slime.

They dug her up, taking all morning and most of the afternoon. A few of the children went off to be sick, and some of the grownups too. One woman fainted, and had to be revived and led home. Nearly everybody felt uneasy about staying to see this gruesome disinterment. She and the other children who lingered felt this way.

By late afternoon it had been confirmed. They took the small, pale body away for the coroner to examine it. There was no doubt, he said later. She was the same little girl who'd never been found since that day when it had been raining, when her mother had seen her that last time.

In fifty years, she hadn't changed.

This was the final thought that had brought the tears, the realization that had sent her and the others home sobbing.

On a rainy day a little girl sank into the slime, choking and dying. Then, for half a century, people came and went, were born and died, houses burned or rotted and had to be repaired or rebuilt, families moved in or out, and new neighborhoods were built as the town grew. Time passed. And all through these years, a little dead girl lay in the back yard behind the Monarch house, her body resting only a few feet underneath the damp soil, not changing, staying exactly the same, waiting to be found.

Other little girls had grown up, had grown old and eventually died. But not her.

She could recall the tone of her father's voice as he talked of all this at dinner that evening, the day they'd dug up the little preserved body from the bog. Nobody had felt like eating.

"I'm going to stay young...forever..."

The dead girl had stayed young for longer than a lot of people had lived their entire lives in the town.

"Stay young...forever..."

The memories turned and changed endlessly.

She wanted desperately to know. Was she lying on her bed, in her room, with summer outside the window, stretched out and sweating with a childhood fever, her head bright with a lump from where it had hit the rock next to the brass dog, her young, smooth face contorted in dream and pain?

She could see it so plainly in her memory, the way her foot came up as she looked down while she was running, the way she slowly tumbled over the hard, heavy body of the brass dog.

She saw her leg slide the wrong way on the slick metal, ever so slowly, and then she was there to see the rock rise slowly up through the tall, cool, fresh, green grass...oh, so vivid!...to crush into her brain like a blunted sledge.

The pain now wracked her entire universe.
And then it swept off and away, a million shrieking needles.
It was gone. She was awake.

Was it summer that she saw? Or winter?
Was it the world she knew and remembered, or was it the frigid loneliness she'd felt each time the black specter had come into her mind? She threw open her eyelids like shutters.

The room was strange in a way she could never have anticipated. Instead of dark, lacquered wood, the walls were featureless and pastel-colored. And the bed was unlike anything she'd ever known or seen. The room was alive with blinking panels of lights. They seemed to be watching her. Hoses and cords dangled everywhere, connected to hidden, throbbing machines on metal racks.

White snow swirled outside the window.
She was seized by a spasm of panic. She twisted from side to side in her restraints, moaning. And this only increased her terror, because the voice sounded exactly like old, decrepit Mrs. Ramsbottom's!

"I'm going to stay young forever!" she croaked.
A white-clad nurse rushed into the room. Her eyes widened in shock when they focused on her. She turned and ran out again, calling for a doctor.

The person in the bed tried to sit up, with great effort. She saw with ever-mounting disbelief that her hands were the gnarled, speckled hands of her grandfather! She threw aside the sheets, and swung around to let her bare legs hang toward the icy floor.

With incredible difficulty, she stood up and fought to bring herself closer to a mirror she could see over a dressing counter, on the opposite wall.

Standing there, she looked for a moment at her reflection. Then she screamed.

The very ogre that had haunted her nightmare opened its black, gawping maw and screamed back.

She lost herself in a pit of darkness.
She never came out of it.
They found her on the floor, dead.
When he finally arrived, the doctor wrote on his clipboard that Dorothy Feldspar, aged 90, had just now come out of her lifelong coma.

Morning and the Rain

The real tragedy was that this, of all mornings, was the most beautiful.

Spring rain fell softly in a world of greens and grays. The trees reached with new life toward the pregnant, steel-colored sky. A cool, moist breeze blew in through the open window, scented with vitality and renewal.

The coffee tasted warmer in the cup, and Alice, Virginia, and my wife Nancy looked more alive and radiant than ever, as we sat together at the breakfast table.

But this was not a morning of beauty, hope, or pleasure.

I saw the feeling of cleverly concealed doom in the eyes of my two daughters, even as they smiled back at me.

I noticed the anguish in Nancy's way of keeping her gaze from meeting mine.

Of course, my wife had been the first one up on this rainy morning, as usual. Her moving about in the kitchen, sending scents of cooking through the cool-shadowed house, had brought the rest of us around. I had risen to a vista of green leaves and gentle rain, and had rushed to dress and join my family.

Nothing seemed changed.

And now we ate, Nancy passing the bacon, eggs, toast and jam around the little table, asking that we all have more.

"Did you sleep well?" she asked me.

It was a false question. I answered it falsely.

"Very well indeed! And what a marvelous morning!" I stretched luxuriantly, reaching out with my arms behind me. "Everything's so cool and clean!"

The farce was over when I saw my daughters' expressions.

We all knew what had happened last night. In the depths of a moonless night, we had been jolted awake in our beds to the sound of sirens, horns, and, I was sure, screaming.

The missiles had streaked flaming across our sky, and had exploded into thunderous billowing hells in the city that lay just beyond the hills to the south.

Who cared who it was? Fanatics with a score to settle against the unbelievers? A psychopathic Asian dictator, wreaking revenge against the innocent? Some renegade Russian faction, trying to use what was left of an abandoned missile arsenal to restore their nation to power?

We heard the dim echoes of the noise, and stood at the windows, watching the blooms of light, bright as sunrise, outlining those ridges, glaring on our faces so that we looked bodiless, corpse-like in our terror. I found myself imagining the death of that city, the sleepers cremated in their beds, stripped of individuality and privacy, suddenly crisped into charcoal as they awoke. Closing my eyes, I could see the panic-stricken, huddling mobs, melting into white-hot slag in their shelters. Then there were the innocent animals who hadn't done anything, waiting in their zoos, stables, and doghouses to be vaporized, not comprehending what was happening even as the sweeping shock waves from the nearby blast reached them, tearing them to pieces, bloody bones and sinews separating, shrieking and howling.

Nancy had trembled and wept. Alice and Virginia had watched with the staring fascination of all children who were unexpectedly faced with atrocity. They were like motorists coming slowly past the scene of a gruesome accident.

And I had left them at their windows and had gone into the nearby upstairs bathroom to be violently sick, as I contemplated our future.

I immediately realized, there in the dark house, that if the city we had always depended on had just died, that the headquarters where I had gone every day to continue doing my job for my country was no longer there, then other cities all around the world were also perishing, bringing civilization to an end.

The era we had known was gone, obliterated in fire. The greed, superstition, and hate which had ruled our world for so long had finally blasted itself away. Mankind's mutual suicide pact had been carried out at last.

We were survivors, all right.

But we were slated for an even worse fate than the billions who had perished in the fire.

We, the remnants, would have to die slowly, achingly, while we watched the dissolution of what was left of our world. As the last trees and the last searching animals died from the radiation, so Nancy, myself, and our children would rot, starve, and die like beasts, crawling eventually into our own futile graves.

I broke down in the darkness, feeling as if I was drowning. A flood of black, apocalyptic horror engulfed me. I looked up at the ceiling, and whatever might be waiting in starry space beyond it, and prayed to that nameless entity of eternity for another wave of flame and fury to sweep down over our suburban valley and cleanse it of us, ending our suffering early.

But death hadn't come.

And here we all were, warm and comfortable the next morning, enjoying another breakfast, celebrating the start of another day.

The farce began anew.

Nancy smiled. "How do you feel this morning, darling?"

"Your cooking is glorious as usual, my dear."

We held hands. She looked at me, love in her eyes.

Alice and Virginia picked at their food, staring toward my wife and me with oversized eyes.

Last night, surrounded by the nightmare, Nancy and I had lain together once again on the bed, in the red-tinted darkness, while a litany of death washed over us from the clock radio on the dresser. Our civilization had indeed ended.

The rest of us who hadn't died in the original blast could only expect to live for another month or so.

And nothing whatsoever could be done.

Nancy had sobbed. "The end of the world – !"

I'd put an arm around her.

"Oh, God damn it!" she'd said mostly to herself, lamenting. "What

125

a sneaky way for those bastards to kill us, to wipe out everybody! What did they think they were accomplishing?"

"They were fanatics," I said flatly. "And fanatics don't care at all about what they do to human beings, just so long as they make their point."

"But what was their point?"

"To prove they were more powerful than the rest of us. To show that they could kill us all if they wanted to."

Nancy laughed. "But a germ can do that. Cancer can do that. Doesn't that mean the people who killed us tonight weren't any better than germs?"

"I'm afraid so." I hugged her tighter. "But we're the survivors now. The world is dying, everything will be a desert soon – "

She moaned. "Don't go on. Please don't go on!"

"But we have a choice," I said. "We're the intelligent ones, not like the plants or the animals. We can do something about what has happened to us. We can fight back."

She rose up, looking at me. "How?"

"We can kill ourselves ahead of time."

"What?!"

"Poisoning," I said.

"But you've always believed so strongly in the value of life, in the necessity of staying alive. Even back when you used to have to be away from home for so long, working for military intelligence or whatever you were working for – "

"CIA, my dear," I said, admitting it at last, because now I knew that it no longer mattered.

"But – " she said, and started to look even more frightened.

"I've saved six cyanide capsules among my things," I told her. "For the past few months it hasn't seemed is if there was anything any of us could do to stave off the inevitable. Too many people working in too many high positions of power, on both sides of the latest conflicts, haven't given a damn about what would happen to the rest of humanity. And I began to worry about the people I loved – "

I held her closer.

"We can't survive this! We mustn't try to outlive what has happened. During the next few years the world is going to degenerate into the bloodiest, most hideous form of hell that anyone with enough of an imagination has ever seen. For people like us, and our children, living will be worse than death. Our daughters are just as important as ourselves. Maybe we can save them from a living nightmare."

"Is it the only way?" she asked.

"I can't think of any other. I will try to arrange for each of us to die as peacefully and comfortably as possible, at least by tomorrow afternoon. You can put two of the capsules into cups of hot tea, and Alice and Virginia will never know."

"Will they just go to sleep?"

"They won't feel a thing. It'll be completely painless."

Nancy embraced me, pulling me down against her. Her body felt hot and tense against mine, her skin sticky with unexpected sweat.

"I want to make love just one last time, before we die," she said.

But I pushed her back.

"What's the point of wanting to create new life when all life on Earth has just lost its meaning?"

She rolled away, onto her side of the bed.

Later, I could hear her softly weeping next to me in the dark.

The following morning, the scenes from last night still haunted me, as I looked at my wife, then got up, pulling my robe on over my pajamas, and moving silently in my slippers through the upstairs, peering at each of our sleeping children in their rooms.

There was so much I could've done to stop this, I thought furiously, squeezing my fists at my side, if I'd only used the opportunities I'd had. I could've misdirected information, made up false reports, misled the military into thinking our position was weaker than it really was. I could've done something.

But I hadn't. I'd let my bosses, and those on the other side, lead everyone directly toward the nuclear confrontation that would end everything. They hadn't cared. And because I was good at following orders, I'd ended up not caring either.

Suddenly I heard someone turning into the driveway outside, pulling up in front of the house.

The radioactive rain continued falling steadily.

Who, I asked myself as I headed downstairs, could be coming here this early?

Through the window beside the front door, I recognized the green no-nonsense Jeep with the tan canvas top which belonged to my aunt Louise, our most obnoxious regular visitor. She was the older sister of Nancy's mother, and ever since Nancy and I had gotten married, she had enjoyed poking her rather long nose into our affairs.

Louise had always been a plan-maker, an organizer of parties and picnics, and trips to the beach. Her two favorite times of the year were the first days of summer, and Christmas.

What was she doing here now, I wondered, after the world had ended?

I moved toward the door to open it and let her in.

"Howard," she said when she saw me, stepping inside.

Today she seemed oddly cowed and humbled. Which, on second thought, was predictable. For someone like her, who'd spent her life thinking about the immediate future, it must've been crushing for her to realize, now, that none of us any longer had a future.

Had she driven the 200 miles from her hometown, upstate, to share these last hours with Nancy and me, and our family? To cry on our shoulders?

As I looked down at her while she pushed past me, I caught myself wondering if I had enough cyanide stashed away to give her some, too. A moment later I realized that my wife was also there, padding down the heavily carpeted stairs.

"Louise," she said, speaking softly enough not to wake the children. They embraced each other.

"Nan, I'm so glad to see you!" Louise said. To me they sounded like a pair of survivors from a shipwreck finding one another in a lifeboat.

Suddenly Louise seemed her old self again, bright, positive, eyes sparkling, her expression seeming to say, 'What will we do for fun and excitement today?'

I followed Louise and Nancy into the breakfast nook in the kitchen, to sit a while with Louise, and talk, while Nancy bustled off across the room to warm a tray of bakery crullers and make coffee. A short time later, Louise excused herself and stood up, disappearing into the nearby downstairs bathroom.

She came out with her face obviously red and tear-streaked, and sat again with Nancy and me in silence, the three of us not knowing what to say next.

Outside the house, trucks and cars kept passing on the street. The cars were piled high with luggage, whole families riding somewhere.

At one point Nancy called my attention to a flatbed truck with yellow government radiation-warning signs on its sides, piled high with zippered, olive-green, plastic body bags.

The children showed up a few minutes later. Seeing them, Aunt Louise suddenly changed back into the children's best friend she'd always been, giving them each her famous, beaming, camp-counselor smile.

She hadn't wanted Nancy and me to see her weeping. It was obviously why she'd gone into the bathroom and shut the door. Now she was putting on a brave front for the kids as well.

Good old, pushy Aunt Louise, I thought.

"I feel wonderful this morning!" she blurted, reaching to touch each of the kids on their shoulders.

Nancy and I both stared at her. Was she serious? Didn't she know what had happened?

"Just think," she went on, looking around at all of us. "Everything's changed. Those who were in control aren't anymore. If the other side's bombs did so much damage to the city here, think of what the bombs we sent over to them in retaliation must've done to their cities, to their army centers, to their bosses and commanders! The whole slate has been wiped clean! All the people who wanted this war have probably been exterminated! They can't do any more to hurt us. They're gone!"

She leaned toward us.

This, I realized, wasn't a false front. She really meant what she was saying. Was this why she'd come all this way?

"Aunt Louise?" Nancy said wonderingly.

Louise focused more directly on her, while our children sat watching.

"We can build a whole new world!" Louise persisted. "This is our chance, for those of us who are left, to make our decisions differently this time, to do things right!"

Outside the sky had turned even darker. The rain fell harder.

I tried to come to terms with Louise's optimism, going on with my original plan, from last night, to kill myself and my family today before things outside could become any worse.

After a while I said, "Excuse me," and got up from the table.

I went upstairs alone. In the master bedroom I dug through my secret cache in the closet, until I found the deadly capsules in their sealed containers. I took them out and held each one as though it was a tiny bomb between my fingertips.

I turned them over. They seemed to change into something much larger and deadlier. Even though I'd been around pills like these since the start of my career, I could almost feel the death seeping out of them, through their hard gelatin coatings.

I came back downstairs, and signaled silently for my wife to get up from the table and come out with me into the front room, so I could show her the capsules.

She embraced me.

"I've thought about it too," she whispered. "And I agree this is the best way. I'm not a survivor. Neither are the children."

I handed her the pills.

Later, she put a pot of tea on the stove to heat. I went out into the dining room, where everybody else had gathered, to announce that we were all going to have some tea.

Louise was becoming increasingly excited about our future. Maybe it was her way of hiding her hysteria, her panic, the fact that she really couldn't do anything at all.

The most dangerous thing was that I could see her manic mood starting to infect the children. They were taking her seriously. They had stopped looking down at themselves, and were paying eager attention to Louise.

"Just think of the possibilities!" Louise looked up at me. "Haven't you ever had an idea you wished you could try out, which might make society better? All we have to do, now, is pool our resources, and there's no limit to what we can do! There's nobody left in charge anymore, to stop us!"

Moving silently behind us, Nancy brought out the tea, taking the cups off the tray and placing them in front of us on the table. There was a cup for Aunt Louise too. I'd found enough pills for all of us. I was sure she didn't want to survive either, no matter how she was raving for the children's benefit.

Suddenly Louise saw the expressions on our faces.

She picked up the teapot, and whirled to smash it against a nearby wall. My daughters stared in shock and surprise. Next, she grabbed each of our cups and splashed the tea from them into a corner.

She came charging around the table and grabbed my shoulders.

"What's *wrong* with you?" she shouted into my face. "What was in those cups, that pot of tea? Tell me!"

I refused to answer her. The silence dragged out.

"Cyanide," Nancy admitted at last. She said it softly, shamefully, under her breath.

"Why, you silly, stupid CIA *spook!*" Louise yelled at me.

I stared at her. How the hell had she found out my true identity?

The sound of her voice cut through the fog of self-pity I'd been feeling ever since last night. "Just because the rest of the world might've wanted to commit suicide," she said, "is that any reason for you to think that life's no longer worth living too, that you've got to follow the people you used to work for down the same tunnel, the same sewer pipe leading to hell?" She cast a brief, apologetic glance behind herself at our two daughters.

Then she faced me again. "You cringing, crawling coward! We've got all *eternity* ahead of us, especially you and your descendants, those of us who are willing to risk staying alive! You're both talented people. Your talents're going to be *needed* during the effort ahead, the struggle to build a new civilization!"

"Louise," I said back to her, "don't you realize it's all over?"

She started to laugh.

"All over? How foolish can you be? It's just beginning! Our greatest adventure is going to be staying alive for the next ten years or so. I'll probably be too old to see it through to the end with you and your kids. But no matter what happens to me, I'll be right there in the grandstands, rooting for you all the way."

I sighed. Just like always, Louise was too much for Nancy or me. How could we predict what she was going to say next? I stared across at her. "God, I wish you weren't so damned optimistic!"

"Aren't you lucky I am!" She pulled Nancy and me to our feet, and put her arms around us. "Come on, let's sit back down here at the table and start making plans." She looked back toward Nancy. "Then I want you both to come out and help me. I brought a dozen things in the car, camping supplies, books, equipment, a generator, cans of gasoline."

An electric feeling flashed through me.

I hardly felt as if I'd ever really known Aunt Louise. This was no game with her. Perhaps everything she'd done with us in summers past, had been for a purpose too. I realized that the government job I'd had until the day before yesterday was nothing compared to the determination I could see in the eyes of this gray-eyed, steely-haired survivor.

"Go back into the kitchen, there, and make some coffee. And boil up some cocoa for these two kids!" she said. She was getting things organized. "Then dig up some pencils and bring some blank writing paper when you come back out here. We've got *plans* to make! There're people I want you both to meet! Take a nap today, the way I'm going to do, all of you. Tonight's going to be a busy night for everyone. I'm going to get on the CB in my Jeep outside, and make some calls. There's so much we have to *do*!"

I began laughing to myself as I left the room. Where had I lost control?

And wasn't it a good thing?

The Segmented Key

Eve Wright felt it as she drifted slowly upward out of a deep sleep into a shallow one, at four in the morning. Her husband couldn't have noticed, because she didn't shift or change position.

What Eve felt was love, a sudden, distinct twinge of love. This intrigued her. She couldn't remember the last time she'd had an amorous dream. She subconsciously inspected the feeling in her sleep. She held it as if it were an object, and explored it with her hands. It was pure emotion, a child cuddling against her chest, Marshall's strong masculine arms gripping her, the silence of a summer afternoon, the licking of her dog Lester's warm tongue on her hand. But it was also more than these.

The dream changed. She saw a deity in her vision, powerful yet friendly, all encompassing yet intensely personal. It was a ray of light from a high mountaintop, a dawn of particular beauty she had seen somewhere that she could no longer remember, the multicolored stipples of a beautiful fish swimming in crystal-clear water, finny and glittery. It was the iridescence of a marvelous insect she may have never seen.

Which was closer to the truth.

The very thing which was causing her emotional explosion, her headlong plunge into love and sensuality, perched but did not perch delicately on the skin of her neck, as though in a reflection from the other side of mirror, not really there. It kissed her tinglingly.

133

*

"There's a door in the sky," she said the next morning at breakfast. Marshall, who never looked up from his crossword puzzle in the paper, looked up now.

"A what in the what?"

She shivered. "Did I say...?"

"A door in the sky," he repeated.

"I must've still been half-asleep. I had the strangest dream last night." She suddenly looked red and upset.

"About doors in the sky?"

"I...don't know," she stammered, taking too big a sip of her coffee. "It was so real! That's what bothers me."

He smiled. "Well, forget it. Especially if it makes you this nervous. It's daytime now, and I have to go to work."

She stiffened. "But that's not important anymore!"

"It is to me. I've a living to make."

"You don't...understand. The door is there, and I've seen it for the first time. I think I'm the first person in the world to ever see it! In a little while, you won't have work to go to! We won't be here anymore. We won't be real anymore. All this has been temporary!"

He got up. "Control yourself, darling. You just had a dream. Now, don't go applying it to everything around you. Nothing's going to change. No bombs are going to fall, no earthquakes hit, no burglaries or fires or plagues." He leaned over the table to kiss her on the forehead. "I'm going to work, and you'll stay here and mind the house, and see that the kids get to school, as usual."

She seemed to soften, the wild look fading from her eyes. "I'm sorry, dear," she said contritely. "I'm all right now. You can trust me."

"That's my baby," he said.

And after he'd gone, she sat at the table waiting for the children to begin waking up in their bedrooms. She could hear the door opening in the sky, over the roof of the house. It made no echo.

"Maybe we should get away this weekend," Marshall said that evening. "The Memorial Day holiday is coming up, and I could get a lovely suite out on the coast, at the hotel my company has a contract with, where we entertain business clients." He looked at her. "What we all need is a break from this routine. What do you say?"

She looked distant. Her mind tried to focus on breakers and the sight of the kids running into the surf for a swim, but all she could see instead was a strange world of emerald towers under a sky that glowed crimson, and she couldn't imagine where such a world might be.

As Marshall continued to outline their possible vacation, she realized that she was indeed obsessed with getting out, getting away. She had an unexpected fascination with traveling very far, into remote and alien places, where no human had ever gone before. She also wanted to be alone, and yet she knew she needed love. She wanted Marshall and herself, and the kids, to travel to someplace very distant and exotic, as soon as possible.

The coast, and the ocean, meant nothing to her, compared to the interstellar distance she pondered inwardly.

The following afternoon she sprawled across the double bed in the master bedroom, the sunlight filtering through the pulled window-shades, golden and warm, giving the room an unearthly, underwater glow. Something racing through her nerves spoke to her. Its voice couldn't be ignored.

The day had gone quietly, and now no breezes rose outside to disturb her calm.

Something keened in the room, hovering near the ceiling. Eve thought it might be the familiar ringing in her ears, which she often heard when things were this quiet.

It eventually went away.

You are a special creature, Eve. When you were born, you were blessed with a secret gift. Because of your power, you can be my lover. You can know me with the love of the universe.

I can take you where we both must go. You have the strength and I have the consciousness to guide you. You make me whole and entire. You are the Ego. I am the Id.

The creature clung among the delicate hairs on the back of Eve's neck. Its proboscis parted like a scissors, a central pipette extending. A tiny jeweled barb slid in through the soft flesh, painlessly piercing. Eve felt it somewhere in her subconscious, and recognized the feeling.

Unrecognizable elements entered her. The thing throbbed on her neck, humming to itself.

She felt love. She felt an all-consuming, all-powerful surge of perfect love, which flooded through her like a tide. She lay still on the bed, face-up, but not noticing the ceiling, gasping with passion. She pulled at her long, dark hair. She moaned, sighed, and trembled along the length of her body. Love enveloped her like a cloud of warm, pink dreams.

A star glowed and flared in a lavender sky, a spectacular star of ultraviolet light, bathing an unknown world in deathly radiance. Crystal things swam through the clear, deep-purple air among a forest of rising, changing, self-transforming crystalline spires. Beings with multiple, faceted, gemlike eyes sought her through undulating webs of light and color, touching and yet not touching her, covering her with tides of potent, sensual pleasure.

This is good, said a voice. It sent a great pulse of ethereal energy into her.

Eve turned over onto her other side on the bed.

A dull red star hovered in a green sky, enveloped by circling strands of rainbow-hued gas. A jungle grew riotously beside a glowing, sapphire-colored lake, the leaves reflecting the star's light and the gaseous loops. Colors Eve had never seen before shone under the leaves. An aquamarine-skinned creature with a tentacle rose up and stretched it tentatively out, fumbling among the thick-bladed ground plants to reach her.

We will go there together, said the voice. Just you and I.

None of the housework had been done when Marshall arrived home that evening.

Dinner wasn't prepared, the food still in the refrigerator. When the kids got home from spending another day of their last week at school, they found Marshall fussing around in the den.

"We're going out tonight," said their mother. She had dressed only in a house dress, and her hair was matted and stringy.

Marshall didn't understand her.

"What did you do all day?" he asked.

She came into the kitchen and sat down at the breakfast table. He joined her there, sitting across from her, peering curiously into her eyes.

"That's just it, darling," she answered. "I don't know."

He fiddled with a cigarette, got it lit, and puffed smoke nervously. "What do you mean, you don't know?"

She sighed, trying to corral her rampaging thoughts. "I remember lying down for a while, but that's all. I simply got tired, and went into the bedroom to lie down."

"And you slept all day, until I came home?"

She shook her head. "No...I didn't. At least, I don't think so. If I'd slept, I would remember dreaming, or feel refreshed, or stiff when I woke up, or something. But I don't remember feeling like that. I feel just the way I did earlier, like..." She paused, still looking at him. "As if the time hadn't gone by at all, and I'd skipped three or four hours completely."

He shook his head.

"Maybe I was just tired," she attempted. "That's it. I was too tired to tell how much time went by."

He eyed her apprehensively.

She gave him a hopeful look. "Do you forgive me?"

He smiled, picked up her hand off the table and kissed it, holding it with his other hand.

"You need a rest, I guess. Let's go out for dinner, like you suggested, whenever you're ready. And I swear we'll take that vacation."

Arrah, this is Eve, our first contact.

Eve, this is Arrah of Ekalad, the Fourth Planet.

She was having another vivid dream that her conscious mind couldn't comprehend.

She and Arrah hovered in a swirling mist filled with thousands of other intelligences. Around them, the landscape shifted, from mountains and forests to an ocean with islands, to a lake in a desert. All of it was beautiful. And all of it seemed unreal.

You are the first human we have found, said Arrah, to possess the true talent, the peculiar mental makeup suited to this next necessary step in the evolution of your race. It is of no consequence that you are a female. You must forget your responsibilities in your waking life and assume the role of envoy between your world and ours.

Arrah's mind touched hers the way two different-colored beams of light might touch, shining through a mist. His thoughts wrapped around her, while she could feel herself poking and prodding at his emotional center with hers.

The being who had made the introductions floated in the air next to her, with only the keening tone to signify its presence.

Although we are sure we will eventually locate more humans in your world which possess your inherited talent, for now you have a unique value. It is within your ability to perform the task for which we have contacted you. You are probably the most important person in your planet's history.

We know that your people have improved both in the physical and the psionic planes, making your greatest strides in only the last fifty years. You are now on the verge of vaulting to the stars, at great expenditures of physical energy.

There are conflicts among the various nations on your planet. Their only meaning to us is that they constitute a threat to your further improvement. They waste too much of your potential.

You are building too many mechanisms to do your work for you, taking the quick and easy road rather than exercising and developing your genuine talents. This acceleration of technology will rob you of your chance to rise toward higher levels of existence. It can lead to the annihilation of your race. This is all-important to us, as there are too few truly promising cultures in the galaxy. We cannot stand idly by while a very obviously worthwhile species takes the risk of obliterating itself through misuse of the very power which could instead be used so fruitfully.

We owe a responsibility to your people, to lead you upward rather than letting you slide back into oblivion. And so we have decided to bequeath to you, at this present stage of your history, the powers for which you so uncertainly seek, as a gift. We know that with our assistance you can ascend to your deserved greatness.

Eve listened.

She understood Arrah more than she had assumed she could. And she felt that same aura of love surrounding her as the entity she'd been touching turned, taking its leave, and vanished like a shadow into the brightness of a sun-dazzling scene of lawns, fountains, and gardens in a marble courtyard she hadn't seen before.

Her vision lingered for another moment, then rippled like the reflection on a freshly-disturbed pond. The keening in her ears told her of that other presence, her interpreter. She moved slowly into wakefulness, and sat up.

"I don't know, Dr. Mathers," said Marshall Wright. "She just sits. Sometimes she'll drift away even while I'm talking to her. The children are noticing it too. She'll be talking to them, and then suddenly it's as if she's somewhere else. And her eyes take on that familiar glazed look."

The psychiatrist leaned forward, behind his desk. "About all I can suggest," he said, "is that you start watching her actions more carefully, and write down what you see. Report to me next week, and tell me just what has happened with her. But above all, don't act suspicious. She may be on the verge of something, but we don't want to set her off."

An appointment was arranged, and Marshall turned to leave. Pausing, he went back to the inner office, knocked on the door, and opened it.

"Doctor, you don't suppose," he said worriedly, "that it could be anything dangerous, this thing with my wife, do you?"

"No," said Mathers. "Strain affects different people differently. Maybe she's going through an early change of life. Perhaps she's been taking sleeping pills lately, and they're affecting her." The man sat back in his chair, his arms folded behind his head. "But whatever it is, I'm sure that the two of us, working together, can figure out the cause, and affect a cure."

Marshall arrived home as usual, and found his wife in the bedroom once more. He had been finding her in the bedroom for two months straight, and it was beginning to erode his faith in psychiatry. No woman reverted so suddenly to self-imposed infancy without a reason.

She didn't want to take any vacation, didn't want to help with the kids now that they were home for the summer, or help with the house, or with doing anything else for that matter, anymore.

It had been two weeks since she'd ceased trying to explain away her inactivity, and now she barely spoke to him at all. In fact, there didn't seem to be anything he could talk about with her these days. Nothing that thrilled or enticed or excited her out of her lethargy. She reacted to everything he said and did with the same strange detachment, as if she simply didn't care anymore.

This is your legacy, your endowment, said the voice in her brain, and a fire raced through her consciousness. Her mind became a separate spirit, floating away into a different environment. She felt renewed love, as she had so often lately, and wrapped herself around it with ecstatic recognition.

It was a feeling of connection.

Lately, she'd realized how long she'd been dreaming about finding this emotion, anticipating it. She'd been looking forward to it all her life, since she was born. She was as real in the world of her afternoon dreams as she was the rest of the time in her own world. And yet she was two different people, a wife and mother, but also a sparkling white thing of purest mentality. She was a fire burning with two fuels.

Your race, Arrah said, has come from superstition to logic, from the morbid to the sublime. And yet you remain beings of flesh, bone, and hunger. You are still chained to your animal functions and animal instincts, when you need to be free. You are prisoners of your bodily forms, enslaved in your physical natures. If your physical shapes are disturbed, your mental processes cease. If your mentality is disturbed, your physical self lingers on, dominating you, in a painful and doomed existence. This is the fate of all naturally-evolved creatures. You are the children of the molecules that made you, the chemical reactions inside your bodies, which you inherited from your planet's primordial birth.

You have come as far as you can, while retaining your link to matter. You have grown from brainless one-celled protozoa in an ancient ocean to beings with brains, and minds, capable of abstract and philosophical thought. You are ready to leave your planet and enter the universe. But here is your problem.

You are still molecular.

You must obey the laws of physics. You must suffer the affects of the gravity that saves you from gasping to death in space. You have no choice. You cannot travel faster than the speed of light, as long as you remain actual and physical. You cannot know your mentors in the other regions of the cosmos, unless you stumble blindly along the only pathways open to you among the stars, spending your meager lifetime traveling in fabricated vessels with limited power and fuel, enduring the tragedy of time-dilation, condemning yourselves to an uncertain future while denying you the possibility of ever returning home.

Your physical existence is something your race no longer deserves. But there is an alternative.

You need not, and will not, continue to suffer this curse. The need for war is over. Famine and oppression are no longer necessary. The powerful among you will no longer be able to hold the rest of you hostage to their desires. You can indeed enjoy the precious freedom of our company, on the psionic level, which we have decided to give to you and your race.

Here is the power.

Arrah held out something which changed in front of Eve's eyes into a tool, and then a jewel of dazzling glory. It suddenly dissolved, its light sweeping through into her mental core, filling her with a longing to wander, to explore, to learn.

The light was pure disembodiment.

"Mrs. Wright," said Dr. Mathers. "I only want you to answer my questions. Please tell me whatever you can about what you've been experiencing. But don't try to make me understand. Simply open up what is apparently locked inside your mind."

The woman, whose hair had begun to turn gray at the temples, after three months of intensifying near-catatonia, who was so thin that her clothes no longer fit properly, lay prone on the couch, listening.

Marshall sat across the room, sadly contemplating what had once been a vibrant, aware, sensible woman. The psychiatrist sat behind the couch, a tape recorder running quietly at his elbow, a notepad and pencil poised in his hands.

"Who are you?" he asked.

"Eve Adams Wright."

"What do you think of your husband?"

"I love him."

"Have you been having nightmares?"

"The door in the sky has opened."

"What door, Mrs. Wright?"

But the voice buzzed and keened around the edges of her consciousness like a dream.

You are the only one, it said. We still haven't found another. You can lift your race out of the trap of the physical world. You can rescue your race. This is your promise, the gift you inherited from eternity.

They sat together in the reception room. A white-uniformed intern stood off to one side. Eve Wright looked at her husband for the last time. She was being committed.

The institution was small, and very expensive. Marshall wanted his wife to have the best care. He still loved her.

She regarded him with the weary, haggard, heavy-lidded look she'd been giving him so often lately. She seemed not to see him directly, but to be looking at him from around an invisible barrier, through a nonexistent fog.

"Take care of yourself," he said.

"I've never stopped loving you," she said with sudden, surprising clarity.

He took hold of her hand. "I know you'll get better. We're all rooting for you."

He almost wept.

A voice inside her head suddenly said –

Now!

A vast chord of orchestral power and intensity burst into Marshall's awareness. His brain seemed to swell with it, pressing against the inside of his skull. He jumped to his feet, startled, unable to find the source of the glorious sound.

At the same time Eve also stood up, clutching at her head, her mouth gaping open, screaming. She collapsed, falling toward the floor. He leaped forward to catch her.

Eve's eyes were still open, but were fatally glazed, as a crew of interns rushed over to take hold of her. They carried her into a nearby room, where they deposited her on a padded table.

A short time later a physician came in to examine her.

It took only a few minutes for him to determine beyond a doubt that Marshall Wright's wife was dead.

*

Eve was flying.

That was the only way she could describe what was happening to her. She floated only a few feet over the rooftops, heading home to her husband and children. It was a brilliant moonlit night in late August. Nightingales and mockingbirds sang in the trees.

She drifted horizontally, face-forward, her feet sticking out behind her. She seemed to be wearing clothes, but she couldn't feel anything covering her body. The essence of what she had become was barely visible, streaming through the empty air like the palest mist.

The sensations she felt were so exquisite that she nearly cried out for joy. It hadn't been a death at all, but an awakening, her eyes opening onto a beautiful new existence.

She remembered how she had felt during the last days of her mortal life. It had been a tragic period, filled with uncertainty, while she waited to hear the voice of the keening sound which would give her the signal to contact her husband with the power.

She was almost home now. She recognized familiar streets. It was like focusing in on something with a powerful telescope. First she had been floating over the entire planet, seeing its oceans and continents rotating below her as if it were a toy. Then she had swept inward, toward the cloud-streaked surface, breaking through the clouds and approaching her home. Now she could see such details as the leaves on the trees, the grass on the lawns, and the shingles on the roofs.

She dropped down on a warm breeze in the early hours of a late-summer dawn, bathed in the full golden light of the moon which was sinking toward the west.

And she easily entered her home, seeping invisibly through the roof and walls with all the actuality of a radio signal.

Marshall had finally gone to sleep, after spending several hours thinking about what he was going to do next, about keeping his job, while taking care of the house. The children weren't here tonight. He'd sent them to stay with his younger sister and her husband, at their place across town.

Despite the months his wife had been sick, her death had still taken him by surprise. He felt abandoned. She had died after touching his hand. And now the eager girl with whom he had fallen in love, who he had known for a third of his life, was gone. Her body waited in a mortuary not far from here, for a funeral which he would attend only to help her into the ground. A vision came to him of himself gently assisting her while she stepped carefully downward through the grass, in the middle of some alien ruin. He saw the late-afternoon sun, and felt the anguish tightening in his chest, and gently, ever so gently, he held her small hand in his.

He pushed back the unwanted dream, and rolled over onto his other side, facing the opposite wall of the bedroom.

Suddenly a spirit was there beside him, a warm presence. He reached out toward it in the darkness, and wondered at what he thought he was touching.

He knew it was Eve. He turned back and caressed her. She was real. A rush of love washed over him. A strange yearning unexpectedly filled him.

He got up without turning on the lights.

The neighbors didn't realize that something was wrong until three days later.

The coroner put down the death of Marshall Wright to stress brought on by acute grief. He'd missed his wife's funeral.

Arrah greeted Norman Williams, the secretary-general of Earth's United Nations. The meeting, anticipated for fifty Earth years by the population of Ekalad Four, was an occasion for dignified celebration.

Throngs of multicolored entities floated up through encircling rings of perfumed atmosphere and thought-force, singing. Minds touched and mingled, dancing around each other in appreciation.

The federation's leader, Amak Bo-Varah, changed shape and billowed toward both Eve and the human official. They came into more intimate contact with each other.

Williams assumed his former human shape long enough to extend a hand in diplomatic friendship. Amak Bo-Varah formed himself into a similar shape, and the two men shook hands formally, like gentlemen.

"Welcome to our federation," said Bo-Varah.

"I am honored," Williams replied.

"On this day, a new order has come to humankind."

"All thanks to the work of Eve Wright," Williams acknowledged, turning his head to smile at her.

Having taken her old shape herself, standing alongside an equally human-looking Arrah, Eve returned the smile.

"Yes," said Bo-Varah, "her and Arrah, and those other pioneering humans who were brave enough to give up their bodies to receive the power."

"All humanity wishes to express its deepest appreciation and fond gratitude to the federation for this gift."

A vast cheer went up from the clouds of other consciousnesses which surrounded the small group, witnessing this ceremony.

It had been a hard-fought transformation, Eve recalled. The living had mourned the dead. Then came the efforts of the scientists, and the military, to stop what seemed to be a worldwide plague.

The physical inhabitants of Earth had turned to violence and superstition to combat what they could see happening. Scapegoats were hunted down and tortured. As the cities, towns, and villages of the world's nations emptied out, the dwindling numbers of survivors had gone mad, sweeping through the streets in mobs, burning homes and scouring the countryside for victims.

Earth's animals had suffered the worst, being unable to join the departing ghosts heading for the next dimension, yet suffering the brunt of the panic on the part of the living. By the time the transformation of the humans was complete, many species, who were destined to inherit the empty planet, had shrunk to a few struggling individuals hiding out in pockets of remaining wilderness.

Also, Eve hadn't forgotten the keening spirit who had first given her the feeling of love, whose identity still mystified her.

After the ceremony was over, she and Arrah dissolved, and met privately in the upper layers of Ekalad's shimmering atmosphere.

Let me introduce you to the agent, Arrah said. The tiny, gemlike insect approached. It ballooned, transforming itself into a woman of dazzling loveliness.

"Hello, Eve," she said. "I am Sharra, originally from the planet Moruela, which we Moruelans have always called the planet of love."

"I'm so glad to meet you at last," said Eve, momentarily becoming herself again.

"How would you like to join me and my fellow agents?" Sharra said. "We can always use new people who are willing to go out to emerging worlds and make first contact."

Long afterward, somewhere else in the universe, Eve once again heard the thin, almost inaudible keening sound. Only this time it was coming from herself. She was making the music of love, which Sharra had taught her, singing a song of private joy and exaltation.

Her high keening carried on the luminous afternoon air along a suburban street, at the edge of a sprawling city, on a planet whose inhabitants had invented mechanisms the same way Earth's humans had done, in their effort to evolve closer to where they could lift off into space.

This was another race of increasingly intelligent, thinking beings, who were tied down by their physical surroundings, to a foreshortened life of limited opportunities, pain, hunger, psychosis, disease, and the unending stress of frustration. She felt an intense urge to begin the process of rescuing these people from themselves.

She moved toward the single candidate which she had found so far, who was the most likely to be the first one of its race to allow itself to be transformed, who in this case was a little golden-haired boy playing on the grass in front of his house.

As she touched him, he glanced up, his eyes wide with surprise and momentary confusion.

Then, once again, another creature in the universe felt the first flooding surge of perfect love.

The Lascivious Ghost

Arthur Tokay was independently wealthy. He was also lecherous. As the sole heir to his family's industrial fortunes, he controlled enough investments to keep him from having to worry about expenses, even large ones, for the rest of his life.

He'd nevertheless grown to be a cynic by nature. A long time ago he'd believed briefly in such trifles as affection, loyalty, and love. But now all he had left was lust. He lived a reclusive life. He'd had it with the world. He had become a cynic because of his sixty years of exposure to all the trickery and hypocrisy of the human race.

As a much younger man, he'd pursued a great number of girls, mostly from the better families. The ones who had simply spurned him, he'd left alone. Others, who tried to change him, he took special delight in ruining. He got them interested in the high life, in drugs and liquor, and introduced them to destitute, yet ravishingly handsome gigolos.

The few he really loved, who became devoted to him in return, he destroyed.

There were some violent scenes. The mother of one girl committed suicide. The father of another came after Arthur with a pistol, and he had to shoot the man in self-defense.

For a while Arthur entertained the romantic notion of perhaps founding a new dynasty with an older, wealthy woman, in suitably lavish style. But the idea quickly bored him.

And so Arthur Tokay grew old as a bachelor. With age, he also grew increasingly ugly.

As his sexual powers, once prodigious, gradually atrophied, his desire for surrounding himself with girls intensified. Arthur turned to being a voyeur, a fondler, an admirer of girl-flesh. Some women were easily conquered. But he wearied quickly of their brainless banality and threw them rudely aside. For a while he joined a group of nudists, until he was driven off by their prim, almost Puritan attitudes. To compensate, he retreated even further into his private world of lasciviousness. He held parties and soirees to which he invited the most nubile females, eager young starlets and fashion models. Beforehand, he had cameras installed in the bathrooms, a secret viewing area built under the swimming pool, and see-through mirrors put in the dressing areas.

He acquired a collection of rare pornography, paintings and incunabula, and wore out his eyesight poring over the films, books, and pictures late at night.

As was inevitable, Arthur became obsessed with possessing the world's most delectable girl.

Hiring agents, he waited while they scoured various countries, sending him back pictures of prospective candidates. The photos were extremely revealing. He spent as many hours studying them at leisure as he'd previously devoted to his erotica. Eventually he spotted the ultimate prize.

Arthur's cynical attitude was reaffirmed as he tried to have her tracked down. At each turn she seemed to elude him. His hirelings ran into numerous obstacles in their struggle to capture the world's most ravishing beauty.

Finally, his luck seemed to triumph over the odds. The quarry was run to ground at an exclusive resort, and Arthur took up residence not far away.

Momentarily setting aside his cynicism, he decided to court her as he would've done if he were much younger, hoping to win her love and affection as well as complete control, in the end, over her delectably spectacular body.

Without meeting her, he inundated her with gifts of flowers and baubles, boxes of candy and rare perfumes. He watched her activities for hours on end, from a distance. Through intermediaries, he paid her compliments and asked to see her. At last, in a note, she agreed to spend an evening with him.

In rapture, he prepared himself for a night of conquest.

When he met her at sunset, in one of the area's most elegant restaurants, his elderly heart began thudding sluggishly with excitement in his collapsed chest. She wore an elegant gown which pushed her youthful bust-line forward while accenting her hips and showing off her slender waistline. Her creamy breasts, nearly exposed to the nipples, jiggled enticingly. Her golden hair shimmered where it draped down in luscious waves into her shoulders. Her eyes sparkled. Her face was a flawless cameo.

But with the first actual view she had of him in return, she was repelled. She tried to cover up her shock at his appearance with a display of politeness. However, he wasn't even able to get through the first course of supper with her. His wrinkled face and leering eyes were simply too much to bear. She excused herself from the table, and didn't return.

He was devastated.

Although he'd known that he was Arthur Tokay, world-renowned bon vivant and lecher, he hadn't thought that his true nature showed so plainly. Thoughts of Dorian Gray plagued him. If only his true looks could've been confined as well to a painting in an attic...

He returned home early to his suite, determined to end it all. Why, he thought bitterly, should he go on living? What was there to live for, if he could no longer be with beautiful women? On his nightstand was, among other things, a large quantity of barbiturates. He was a cynic once more, with a vengeance.

He was through with humanity. Finished. Washed up. His last hopes had been shattered. He would take the pills, go to sleep, and end his dwindling debauchery before being forced to endure any further humiliations.

Undressing, he got into bed and lay back. Soon the pressure of eternal darkness began to close gently in.

Because of his cynicism, Arthur hadn't thought there'd be an afterlife.

When he opened his eyes and looked around the room, he immediately assumed that the fistful of sleeping pills hadn't worked. He stood up, turning and reaching for the empty bottle. He couldn't get a grasp on it. His gnarled fingers went through it without even feeling it. Neither could he pick up his empty drinking glass.

He turned and glanced down at the bed.

There he lay, his complexion gradually turning a dull gray.

So that was it, he thought without rancor. He was a ghost.

He spent a while accustoming himself to this new fact. Of course he couldn't switch on the lights. But he didn't need to. He could see adequately by the lingering glow of dusk outside the windows. He strolled about the room, peering into the empty mirrors until he convinced himself that he had no reflection.

A thrill of excitement flashed through him. He was invisible!

Then, nonchalantly, he sauntered out through the solid wall and paused, standing fifty feet above the early-evening traffic on the boulevard, surrounded by cool night air. His elation grew. He could go anywhere! Walls and locked doors meant nothing to him! The ladies' showers and restrooms of the world were his to explore at last! He could indulge his lechery at leisure.

Walking back into his room, he did a little dance.

Maybe he could still spend some time ogling the world's most gorgeous girl. She would never suspect!

He didn't even notice the dark gentleman sitting in the armchair behind him. Not until he smelled the sulfur.

He turned.

The gentleman smiled. His teeth, like his eyes, were red.

"Hello, Arthur."

Arthur stared. "You can see me?"

His visitor nodded.

"Who are you?"

"A fiend." He chuckled, reaching into the empty air in front of himself. His fingertip caught fire, blazing horribly. He pulled it back, bringing with it a lit cigarette which he proceeded to puff, inhaling deeply. Arthur didn't see the point of panicking. It would only please the fiend, and he looked pleased enough already.

"Nice trick," he commented.

"Yes, isn't it," said the other, blowing smoke. "Nasty habit, though. Want to break myself of it."

"Well, get to the point," said Arthur impatiently. "What are you doing in my room? What business have you got with me?"

"I've come to take you along. Got word of your intended suicide just now, and I took the least amount of time possible getting here. We have an appointment."

Arthur backed apprehensively away. "Where?"

"You know where. You've known since you were thigh-high to a dancing girl."

"I suppose I have," Arthur admitted. "Is it really as bad as everybody says?"

"Oh, I don't know about that. There are a lot of interesting people to meet."

"But," Arthur said, deciding to try bargaining, "I have something else I want to do first. Do you mind? A sort of last wish, you might say."

"Very well," said the fiend. "I suppose I might as well allow you this one indulgence. What do you wish to do?"

"Pay another visit to the lady I took to dinner earlier. Maybe I can get there soon enough to watch her disrobe before she retires."

Although he was as cynical as ever, he was certain that the girl would be as fabulous a sight naked as she'd been fully clothed.

The ghoul sat back. "Ahhh, that should be pleasant."

On their way to the girl's hotel, Arthur said to his equally invisible companion, "I regret that this is my final opportunity to indulge my baser pleasures. As you probably know, my good fiend, I take rather a bit of pride in my callousness. I should've been a doctor, the way I enjoy poking and staring at the various intimate features of girls' bodies. It's a pity that I won't be able to use my newfound ghostliness to do some really extended peeping. A tremendous pity."

The demon looked sideways. "I might have a proposition for you concerning that. I don't see why you shouldn't remain here on Earth for as long as you please. After all, your sins are my pleasure."

"Do you really mean that?" Arthur was ecstatic. He felt his cynicism fading again on a wave of lustful anticipation.

"Of course," said the demon. "Providing that you obtain true pleasure in viewing our little beauty tonight."

"Oh, I will," said Arthur, rubbing a pair of nonexistent hands together. "I promise I will!"

Coming through the wall of the building, they stood in the girl's boudoir. She had just entered from the parlor, after having turned out the rest of the lights in her suite. She was obviously preparing to disrobe.

"Just in time!" cackled Arthur.

Emboldened by his invisibility, Arthur moved closer to the delectable creature, eyeing her hungrily.

Standing at her floor-length dressing-room mirror, she reached back to unzip her evening gown, letting it slide down so that she could step out of it. Picking it up, she put it on a hanger and placed it in the closet. Next came her slip, then her garter belt. Her brassiere followed.

Arthur was in seventh heaven.

The fiend behind him only smiled.

Moving over and sitting down on a small sofa, she unrolled her nylons. Then she stood up again. Arthur wanted to touch her, but the fiend pulled him back. Arthur was breathing heavily now.

Next, the girl took off her wig.

"So she's bald," Arthur remarked. "She's still lovely, even though she's bald."

The girl pulled one false rubber breast away from where it had been attached to her chest with adhesive. It continued to jiggle as she set it down on her bureau. Then she removed the other. Her upper torso was revealed as being as flat and bony as that of a 97-pound weakling, male variety.

Feeling defensive, Arthur still insisted she was lovely.

When she removed one artificial leg, he wasn't so sure.

She sat down and spent several minutes in front of her vanity, taking off her makeup. She had dentures, false eyebrows and lashes, and, to Arthur's horror, a glass eye. Her face, devoid of its covering, was a nightmare of crisscrossing lines and crow's feet.

Arthur could stand it no longer.

"That *does* it!" he cried. "I'm *through*! You *win*, you fiend! You can take me wherever you *want*. I don't care. Women are a *fake*, a *fraud*, a conspiracy to drive men *insane*! I should have *known*! This is the last time I'll *ever* trust anybody! Why was I foolish enough to think that this witch was going to be any different from all the *others*?"

The demon was grinning as it led him back through the wall.

The girl watched them leave. She could see them both with perfect clarity.

When they were gone, she extended her hand. One of her fingers blazed. She brought back a lit cigarette.

Of Another Yellow Summer

It was the evening news.

"In the war today, our forces advanced three hundred more miles into the enemy jungles, sought and destroyed eighteen of their bases, eliminated several villages which had been known to contain sympathizers, and sustained only light casualties. The enemy's losses amounted to several thousand killed, and nearly a million wounded. More action on the front is expected tomorrow, and we will have full-color reports.

"The draft lottery was stepped-up today by Congress. It is estimated that next month's quota will total more than 300,000 under the age of eighteen. This step was necessary, the Defense Department said, to replace the million-plus men lost in action so far this year.

"On the home front, the Post Office has just enacted new legislation which will make it a felony offense to use in private correspondence any of the 235 words already on its official list of 'objectionable language.' The penalty will be the same as that for mailing 'obscene' printed matter or booklets. The Postmaster General called the new law a 'milestone in public morals.'

"In Georgia and Alabama, repeated skirmishes are continuing between Black Panther guerrillas and the Ku Klux Klan. The Panther-held city of Macon suffered its thirteenth consecutive day of massive raids by fleets of Klan bombers, and Mobile was the scene of yet more

155

Panther atrocities as an additional two hundred Klan hostages were executed, to force the surrender of the Klan concentration camps at Birmingham. We will have a special one-hour report on the conflict following tonight's regular late-evening news.

"In geriatrics today, the National Medical Service reports that it is now possible for our older citizens to live to the ripe old age of 250, under complete care in the new Government dormitories. With all of the daily advances in controlling the aging process, the director of the research facility stated that he didn't see why people shouldn't soon expect to see three hundred. Also, according to the report, what with the new artificial-reality headsets, reaching such extreme age will not mean missing out on the latest entertainment. It looks like a long, long future for all of us.

"And there's good news in the pollution picture. A new method has been found for dealing with the ever-increasing problem of refuse and garbage. The proposal is to fill in the Arctic Ocean, layer by layer. An incidental bonus of this plan will be the gradual restoration of our sea levels to their original height, where they were before we began to use seawater in our fusion reactors.

"The crime rate has been determined for the second half of this year. According to the Bureau of Crime Measurement, the average citizen stands a 60-percent chance of getting mugged before next January, a 40-percent chance of being burglarized or vandalized, 30-percent of being molested or attacked, 20-percent of being seriously wounded, 10-percent of being murdered. Another 450,000 persons are expected to die in vehicle accidents.

"Now for the weather. Winterlike conditions will continue for the forseeable future. The sun may come out for a full two hours tomorrow, provided the temperature inversion doesn't lower, and it has been predicted by the weather office that schoolchildren will have a one-hour play period without their smogmasks, between one and two P. M. There should be no pollution alert between nine tonight and four in the morning. Temperatures will remain unseasonably low, the highs expected to rise to only – "

But the newscaster didn't finish his line, because Donald Norton had gotten up from his chair and had just now shut off the 48-inch telescreen. The musty room became very dark.

Norton, in his early nineties, made his creaking way back to the chair, and lowered himself painfully into its depths.

"Couldn't stand another minute of that," he said.

In an adjoining chair, his wife Lydia sat, her eyes swinging from the dead screen to focus on him.

"Why not?"

"Because that isn't our world. It isn't mine, anyway. Look around us! Did we grow up in this kind of civilization? Look at this apartment of ours. This is our world, what's left of it. Not that nightmare out there..." He pointed his palsied finger at the screen.

"Well, my goodness—!" said Lydia, amazed.

"I'm sorry." He spoke now in a lower voice. "But I'm not going to take back what I just said. The world isn't the same anymore. It's turned into something people our age weren't meant to comprehend. Wars! Bombings! Atrocities! Obscenity laws! Pollution! Science gone mad! Let the youngsters have it. I don't even want to hear about it!"

Lydia, still amazed, didn't offer an argument. Donald sat back in his chair, and quietly took stock of his surroundings. Now that the video wasn't on, the room appeared genuinely comfortable. The apartment he shared with his wife was a set of smallish cubicles, in a stolid old building, with thick old-style walls and real wooden floors. Many generations' worth of trinkets and heirlooms lined the place like a nest. Delicate vases stood on inlaid-wood end tables. Lamps of a dozen designs filled odd corners and flanked both the radiant-flame heater and the screen. Books littered tables and lined ceiling-high cabinets. Rugs overlapped on the floor, which squeaked gently when you walked on it. Smaller rugs lay atop worn places in the older rugs underneath. Without a doubt, this room and the kitchen, bedroom, and closet-like bath beyond comprised home.

"You don't have to watch just the news, you know," said Lydia at last, breaking the silence.

"The other shows aren't any better. No matter how loud the laugh tracks are, the comedies always leave me crying, or furious. No matter how thrilled everybody seems to be on the game shows and the quiz shows, how much they jump up and down like children, and clap their little hands, I never learn who wins because I'm always asleep by halftime. The adventure shows make me want to root for the natives, or the crocodiles, and I always have the detective shows puzzled-out before the first commercial. Donald sneered. "No, Lydia, I would much rather read a good book."

"Whatever you say, dear." She shrugged, and reached for one of the many battered volumes stacked next to her chair. Once she'd gotten into that chair, she didn't like leaving it until bedtime, barring major emergencies. It was simply too inconvenient to struggle to one's feet, and then struggle back into the chair again.

While she absently turned pages, Donald leaned back.

"I've been thinking," he said to nobody in particular, "about the past. The good old days. About how things used to be." He took a tired breath and let it out. "How different they were!"

He glanced sideways, but Lydia was pretending to read.

So he returned his gaze to the ceiling, and to his dreams.

"It was a bit of poetry I read the other day," he said absently, "that brought it all back. Something about a yellow summer. All of a sudden I could see everything, just the way it was when I was younger. Do you remember the way the trees used to look, all green and thick with leaves that rustled in the breeze? And what about the sky in those days, so clear and faraway, so that from an upstairs window you could look out and see all the way to the horizon? Remember the lawns? And the big old houses people lived in, with open verandas that looked out onto the rest of the world, not closed-in, but greeting their surroundings like open arms? And the children! Playing games in the yards. Then running off to school, and finally growing older and getting married. What a wonderful time it was! A time for taking deep breaths of the clear morning air, for going on long walks after dark, listening to piano music coming from a house here and there along the way. For riding a bicycle!"

His expression grew even dreamier.

"I could remember our family, my brothers and sisters, Mother and Dad, the aunts, the uncles, the grandparents...It wasn't like it is now, with everyone shut up in separate cubicles, afraid of each other, like strangers. Back then, people lived together, talked together, shared their joys and their problems. And the things we did! The picnics we went to, the socials, the carnivals and the county fairs! What about the circus, and the matinees on Saturdays, and the vaudeville shows? When was the last time you or I tasted a hot dog on a bun, or cotton candy?"

Donald's voice, a reedy rasp, trailed off into stillness. "How I wish I could live in those times," he finished at long last, "just as I am now. But transplanted, as it were, from here to the far-preferable past..."

Lydia continued reading. But eventually she closed the book and looked across at Donald.

"There's something you still haven't realized," she said.

"What's that?"

"We can't change reality."

There was a silence.

"What I mean is, you can't have the world you want, no matter how badly you want it, if it isn't there. All the wishing you do won't make it so."

He looked at her. She was planted solidly in her chair. "You've got to accept things as they are, dear," she said, speaking as gently as she could. "I know you're a dreamer. That's why I married you. It's why I've always loved you. But when it comes to facing the way things are..."

"I can dream if I want to," he said stubbornly. "If I want to create a time machine that'll take me back to better years and a more beautiful world, I will. Even if it's only in my imagination, and I never leave this room."

"Well, dear, there are no time machines." She chuckled. "But if I know you, and there were such a contraption, you'd be the very first one aboard, and reaching out to yank me on with you!"

Donald remained quiet, holding onto his thoughts.

Lydia put down her book again, later. "By the way," she said, "thank you for switching off the news. You're the only man I know who would think of doing something like that. It's been a lovely evening without it."

Not long after the evening when Donald Norton turned off the screen, he and Lydia were visited by an agent from the Bureau of Retirement.

"Good evening," the man said when Donald let him in. He was a mere lad barely in his thirties, and wore the crisp plastic uniform of a medical inspection officer.

"Are you Mr. and Mrs. Norton?" he asked, consulting an electronic notepad he held in his hand.

Donald replied that they were.

"Very good. May we sit down?"

They sat, and Donald offered the government man some tea, which he refused.

"Our records show that you are both well past the normal retirement age," he said, reading the statistics off his small screen, "that you, Mr. Norton, are a retired factory worker, that your children, numbering two, are both fully grown and living elsewhere, and that you are fully-registered citizens and your taxes are paid-up. Correct?"

Of course it was correct. Both Jessie and Wilomene were long-gone, one living in the midwest and the other on the coast. Donald answered each of the youngster's questions as it was asked, wondering where they were all leading.

The agent wasn't long in reaching the point.

It was time, at last, for Donald and Lydia to move into a dormitory.

"We have beds already set aside for both of you. You'll love them, and I'm sure you'll appreciate the chance to take it easy. The service is absolutely complete, nothing has been left out, and you won't have a worry in the world. There are planned activities if you want them, crafts and hobbies for as long as you have the strength to concentrate on them. And, after that, you'll have full use of artificial-reality entertainment." He put the notepad away in his pocket. "We've decided to send a crew to pick you up the day after tomorrow."

Donald and Lydia were quiet for several seconds. The man from the Bureau of Retirement folded his hands in his lap, sitting on the front edge of his chair, trying to absorb the awkward silence.

"What if we don't want to go?" Donald asked.

The youngster regarded him curiously. "I don't understand."

"If we'd rather stay here, in our own apartment, among the things we've acquired over the years, which still have meaning and value to us, instead of allowing ourselves to be taken away and put in a bed in a stripped-bare, hygienic hospital room, can't we do that? I mean, if Liddie and I preferred just to grow old and die, rather than being kept alive by a cold-blooded machine, a super-iron-lung..."

"But," said the officer, "that's unheard-of. Everybody wants to stay alive! Nobody would rather die than have the chance to live to be 300 years old. It's out of the question. You definitely couldn't be left here, to die."

"But," Lydia put in, "that's what we want. And if it's all right with us, why shouldn't we be allowed – "

"Because," the agent interrupted, "It's simply not done. Now, the arrangement is for me to inform you of our intention to come by for you the day after tomorrow. Actually, although we try to make it sound like a privilege and a favor, it's all been planned long in advance. We need this apartment for another family to use, people who aren't ready to go into the dormitories. There is a shortage of apartments these days. Do you understand now?"

"Do you mean..." said Donald in disbelief, "that we have no choice in the matter?"

The agent nodded, with a sad expression.

"Exactly. I'm sorry."

Donald and Lydia stayed up unusually late that evening, after the young government man had gone, pondering their future.

And when they had finally managed to help each other up from their chairs, moving into the tiny dark bedroom, and into bed, they both lay on their backs, unable to sleep because of thinking.

"What are we going to do?" asked Lydia, speaking to the ceiling.

"We can't let ourselves be taken away and put in a dormitory," he answered.

"We couldn't take any of our things along," she reminded him. "What would happen to them?"

He shrugged. "Be destroyed? Taken to a dump and mashed into the rest of the fertilizer."

She was shocked. "The pictures? The lamps? The rugs? The books? Wouldn't anybody want them after we weren't allowed to keep them?"

"They wouldn't be wanted by anybody else," he said. "Nobody but us knows how valuable they are."

He reached across and patted her lovingly in the dark.

It was the next afternoon, the day before the crew from the Bureau of Retirement was due to show up again, that Donald Norton found himself taking a walk downstairs, outdoors, in the open, in order to clear the hallucinations and disillusionments from his head. Despite the pollution, the traffic and the crowds, he needed to get out.

And so, on the pretext of going to buy some tobacco for his pipe, which he hadn't smoked since he could remember, he said goodbye to Lydia in her chair, and stepped down the three flights of creaking stairs, to the rattling front door.

He was no longer even sure that there was a tobacconist's shop along this particular street. The last time he'd gone looking for one had been years ago. Outside, the noise was much worse than he'd remembered, and the ozone and sulfur fumes were palpably stronger. It seemed even colder and grayer than it had been the last time he'd ventured outdoors, as if winter had closed in even more over the city, the sky a dark lid over the roofs of the buildings.

He walked for the sake of walking, forcing his ancient bones to propel him onward. He assumed an attitude of perpetual falling, tipping his weight from foot to foot, making his way along the gritty, sooty sidewalk.

And, as he passed one particular shop, one of many that he couldn't recall ever having seen before, he heard a strange sound. It was an impossibly reedy singsong, chanting, "Summertime, summertime, summertime...!"

He halted himself clumsily, stood balanced on top of his feet, and turned to face the shop from which the voice seemed to be coming. It looked ordinary enough. APOTHECARY, said a sign above the door.

He went inside. What he saw was a small shop lined with shelves. On the shelves were cans, jars, bottles, and boxes. All had colorful, bright-printed labels, but none seemed to show what they might contain.

"Summertime, summertime..." the voice continued.

He saw no one for several seconds. And then a wizened bronze head peeped up over the counter and regarded him with gold-button eyes like saucers. "Yes sir, what can I do for you? Do you need summertime, perhaps?"

"Was that you," asked Donald, "calling out from in here a moment ago?"

With a twitch and a lunge, the proprietor heaved himself up onto the countertop, and stood facing the old man. He was a dwarf, not more than three feet tall. "Yes," he said. "And I can tell by looking at you, sir,

that you want summertime. That, in fact, you need summertime."
Reaching onto a shelf behind him, he brought forth an aerosol can.
"Summertime, on special, today only. Half-price."

He held out the can with a thrust.

Donald, at first vaguely frightened, became intrigued. "Is this it?" he
said, taking the can. "Summertime?" He eyed the label. "What is this
stuff, a room deodorizer?"

"Oh, most certainly not! It's summertime!"

"But...what?"

The dwarf looked deep into Donald's eyes. "What is summertime to
you? Childhood? Nostalgia? Escape? An end to worry? Well! Whatever
summertime holds for you, you will find it in this convenient little can.
Spray it in the privacy of your own room or office, and summertime will
be yours!" He grinned, and went on. "Special price, today only.
Twenty-five cents."

Donald didn't know why, but the next thing he did was pay the little
man a quarter. He left the shop, holding onto the can.

He made his lonely, plodding way back through the afternoon
crowds to his door, up the three flights of steps, and into his apartment.
He closed the door slowly.

Lydia looked up at him. He moved over and sat in his chair, holding
the can of summertime out in front of himself once again and looking at
it.

"What is that?" she asked. "What did you buy now?"

"I'm not really sure," he replied. "Maybe it's an aerosol spray, or
maybe it's really something else."

She asked him how much he'd spent on it, where he got it, and why,
and he told her about the apothecary and the dwarf. "He told me it was
simply summertime in a can."

"How odd," she said, peering at him. Then she grinned. "And silly."

He returned her look.

"It's cruel of people," she continued, "to prey on the sad wishes of
an old man condemned to be moved into a dormitory, who goes out on
walks looking for escape, grabbing at straws. So this little pirate sold
you a dream in a can."

She snorted, returning her attention to the book she'd been reading.
"Summertime...bah!"

Feeling rebuked and uncertain, Donald went on inspecting the can. The label, printed in looping, swirling, Baroque curleycues, bore only one word: Summertime.

He held a hand cupped over his nose, and sprayed out a little mist from the can. He breathed it.

And it was as if the entire world changed color, like a chameleon. The dim umber walls, the video screen, the bookcases and the heavy drapes covering the room's few, small windows all became suddenly green and yellow and clear crystalline blue.

They became a street in a small-town neighborhood, just as Donald had always remembered it, with green lawns, an overhead canopy of summer trees, cool shade, and tall whitewashed houses with high, narrow windows, domes and cupolas. The tangible actuality of it startled and delighted him. His feet actually sank into cool, moist grass, his nostrils tasted, like wine, the summer air, and he felt certain that if he took a step forward, he would be walking into that other world, free.

When Lydia called him back from the vision, he almost wept. He had the feeling in the back of his mind that he had nearly made it into the past, into the world he'd been so obsessed with, lately. One more second in that world, and he felt sure he wouldn't have been able to come back.

"What were you doing, just now?" she asked.

"I don't know..."

He put aside the can. He found it difficult to recover control over his speech, after what must've been an extremely vivid dream.

"I must've blanked out for a moment."

She stared at him, then shook her head. She had been ready to say something, but now she changed her mind.

The next day, they were both ready for the government crew, both sitting in their chairs, Donald with his can of summertime on the side table, and Lydia with her book.

"We've got to learn to take these things in stride," she said, holding the book open in front of herself although she wasn't able to go on reading it. "It's no use trying to slip off into a fantasy world, to put reality behind you. When you do that, you're only fooling yourself."

He nodded, without wanting to.

All night and all morning, he had been working to gather up enough courage to tell her what had happened to him yesterday, when he'd breathed the summertime-spray into his hand. But, from many years of being married to her, he knew how hard it was to convert her, to change her mind if she didn't want it changed. Lydia was a levelheaded woman, and had been the stabilizing influence in his life since the beginning. And now was no different. Without bitterness, she had already convinced herself that life in a dormitory would be acceptable, if it couldn't be avoided. She would adjust. She didn't intend to flee from it, especially into the mind-altering mist from a cheap spray can.

She was ready.

"It won't be long now," he said, "before the Bureau men arrive to haul us both away."

"No, dear. Not long at all."

"Are you ready, Liddie? Really ready?"

She sniffed. "I'm going to miss my things. That's my only real regret. It took us so many years of living together to end up with these pictures, vases, lamps, rugs, books. It's going to be sad for me to say goodbye to them, never to be able to see them again..."

"You know," he said, touching the can, "it doesn't have to end this way."

"Yes it does," she responded, nodding. "There's nothing we can do."

Donald held out the can of summertime. This was their last chance. He wondered whether the spray would reach clear across to where Lydia sat in her chair. How he wanted her to go back into that warm, sunny neighborhood with him! How she would love the grass, the trees, and the stately old houses!

"Have faith, darling," he said, and pressed the sprayer.

That afternoon in Prairie City, Iowa, the weather was clear and warm. The grass on the lawns was deep and spicy-moist. The leaves of the overhanging oaks and elms rustled in the cool breeze. Somewhere a piano was playing, a tinkly ragtime tune. Children romped near the sidewalk, while older folks sat and rocked in their chairs on the veranda, talking.

Somebody saw Donald, bringing Lydia with him by the hand, coming across the lawn.

"Well, Grandpa and Grandma," they said. "Back so soon from your stroll."

When the plastic-clad workers from the Bureau of Retirement arrived at the Norton apartment to take the two old people away, they found it empty.

Some of My Best Friends Are…

I'm not saying I don't like orangatangs on principle. Or that I wouldn't respect one on a social level at a party. Some of my best friends are orangatangs. They dress well, and are a very cultured people.

And they're great dancers. Nobody can dance like an orangatang.

It's just that I don't like orangatangs in my house. It's a bad enough idea to live next door to one of them.

And I don't like orangatangs going to the same school with my daughter. Little Nell is an impressionable girl, and she is liable to fall for their fascinating ways and their animal charm.

It's not that I don't respect and appreciate all the advances made by modern science. I jumped for joy the day they found that orangatangs could be taught English. I leaped in ecstasy the day they gave an orangatang a job as a clerk. I was one of the first men in my company to have his shoes shined by the orangatang around the corner. I was only too happy to walk up to one on the street and shake his paw.

But the sight of an orangatang in a gray tweed suit with a briefcase applying for a job with our company nauseated me. They're supposed to stay in their place, and eat watermelon, and dance a lot.

But not drive around my neighborhood in fancy sedans, looking for new houses. Or walk around in a gray suit carrying a briefcase.

I think an orangatang looks his best in coveralls.

*

I remember when the trouble started.

I caught Nellie one day listening to that pornographic orangatang music on her I-Pod. She said she liked it, and I took the I-Pod away for a week.

The very next day, my wife told me that an orangatang had been around to read the meter. "He was a very handsome fellow," she said, and I stood aghast. I tried telling her how dangerous it was for human women to go around encouraging orangatangs, but she just went off into a long, tedious lecture about civil rights.

Being not the least interested in such things, I left the house and went down to Red's place to have a quiet drink and get the subject of orangatangs off my mind. Red fixed me up with a double, and then a deep voice said, "Mind if I join you, sir?" beside me. It was a Princeton accent. I turned, and there beside me sat an orangatang, grinning at me with rows of ivory teeth. He was wearing a gray business suit, and his businesslike briefcase sat demurely next to him on the floor.

I left hurriedly, without finishing my drink.

I'll be damned if I'll drink with an orangatang.

The next day, on my way up to my office, I discovered an orangatang in a janitor suit, cleaning the floor near the elevators. I gave him a dime. In the office, I got word that B. G. was calling a meeting of the board of directors, and I spruced up and combed my hair, and took the elevator to the top floor. I took my chair, near the back, and arranged my notes in front of me, in case anybody should want to ask me any questions about my department.

As the others filed in and took their places, I received the cruelest blow so far. Instead of old Ned Hobson, a big burly orangatang took the chair across from me. Like all orangatangs, his arms were twice as long as his legs, and he had to balance on the chair where he was sitting, trying to look comfortable. He smiled at everybody with his big teeth, as though he owned the place. I could only stare.

B. G. introduced him as Osgood P. Fuggs, and announced with the utmost propriety that he was joining the firm as a junior executive. It turned out he had graduated from one of those orangatang colleges that some smart reformers had started down south. He was replacing Ned Hobson.

I couldn't help staring at him as he sat there. His briefcase lay on the table where he'd just put it. I'd never been so shocked in my life! He did everything humans do. He paid attention to B. G.'s hypnotically boring remarks. He looked the part perfectly, the classic executive! Except...have you ever seen an executive with thick orange hair all over his body, wearing a gray flannel suit and Italian shoes?

During the lunch hour, I left the building for a few short ones at a bar down the street, and with my courage thusly strengthened I paid a visit that afternoon to Mr. Farnsworth, the comptroller.

"Where's Hobson?" I demanded.

Farnsworth gave me his standard smile. "Have a seat."

"Has that orangatang named Fuggs replaced him, like B. G. said? I don't believe it!"

"Have a cigar," Farnsworth intoned.

"You mean to tell me that animals can be dragged in here from the jungle and take people's jobs away from them after they've worked here for years?"

"How's your department coming along?" Farnsworth interrupted.

I flung up my hands. "Okay, all right, you win. But no animal from the jungle's going to take my job away from me, nosiree Bob!"

Farnsworth leaned back in his chair, blowing out smoke. "Good cigar, isn't it?"

I gasped. "They can't do that, can they? Take my job away? I got a family to support!"

"You know, cigars like these are hard to get. Have to go to Brazil, you know, to get them."

"We can't let the human being go down the drain! After all, we're still the dominant species on this planet, aren't we?"

Farnsworth puffed. "Far superior to the old Havanas."

"We can't just give everything away to these interlopers, just because some fool taught 'em to speak English!"

Farnsworth swung around to admire the view outside the windows of his corner office. "Nice day, don't you think?"

"I know it's important that animals improve themselves. It was wonderful the way the scientists figured out how to increase their intelligence. But really...!"

"Not a cloud in the sky," Farnsworth commented.

"I know we've all got adjustments to make, but is it fair to force something on people that they don't want? Is it?!" I jumped up. "I don't care what you say! I'm never going to give up my superiority to some damn fool monkey! No matter what happens! I've got my pride. Osgood P. Fuggs may be a nice fellow, but I won't stand for much more of this! Do you hear? I'm not going to stand by while they let these beasts walk all over us humans!"

"Now, what was it you wanted to talk with me about?" Farnsworth asked, turning to focus on me for the first time.

"No sir!" I hollered. "I won't quit without a fight! That goes for Osgood, and all the other orangatangs that move in here!"

With that, I turned and stalked out of the office.

I thought I could hear Farnsworth saying, "Nice talking with you," just before I slammed the door.

"Daddy!", little Nell called up to me from downstairs. I had been taking care of some office work in my upstairs den.

"What is it, dear?"

"I brought a friend home to meet you."

"That's nice." I got up and went into the bedroom for my smoking jacket. I never met any of her school friends without my smoking jacket. When I got to the living room, I staggered backward, almost losing my balance.

Nellie was waiting for me on the love seat, sitting next to the biggest, burliest, hairiest orangatang I'd ever seen outside a zoo. "Hello, Mr. Beemus," he said.

He had on a high-school sweater, with a letter, white shoes, and white Levis. He looked like a cheerleader, albeit one with arms twice the size of his legs.

"His name's Rufus Boomer," Nellie said.

"You!" I screamed, "Get outa my house!"

"Daddy!" Nellie gasped, suddenly trembling, her curls quivering.

"That's all right, honey," the orangatang said.

"Get outa here afore I whop you!" I proposed.

"Yessir," Boomer said, and headed for the front door.

"Yassuh, yassuh massa boss man," I mimicked.

"Daddy!" Nell wailed.

"G'wan, bwah! G'wan an' git, afore I thrash you with a hickory switch!"

The orangatang hurried out.

"And put on some coveralls!" I shouted after him. Then I deftly slammed the front door.

Nellie threw herself on the sofa, weeping.

I sat down beside her. "Dear," I said, "why did you have to bring an orangatang home with you? You know what it does to property values."

Nellie howled.

"We've got to keep up appearances," I continued. "Just think what the neighbors would say."

She wailed and bawled, and covered her head with a pillow.

"You may like that orangatang a lot," I conceded, "but, after all, we're trying to bring you up to be a refined young lady. And when you go out in the world, you're going to have to be respectable."

Nellie lifted the pillow, peered up at me, then resumed blubbering.

"You're going to have to maintain your elegance and sophistication," I said. "We are an upstanding family, and it just wouldn't do for you to be seen fraternizing with the lower classes, now would it."

Nellie didn't seem to be listening.

"Nellie," I said, "please promise me you won't bring any more orangatangs here to the house."

"Oh, Daddy!" she caroled.

I finally stood up and went to find my hat. Perhaps the evening would be better spent at Red's, over a few highballs.

Kids just seem to be getting harder to talk to these days.

When Alma served the meat loaf that evening, it was cold. Sounds of sobbing were coming from Nellie's room upstairs. They had been coming from there since I'd walked back from Red's place.

"Looks good," I said, picking up my fork. It wasn't clean, as usual. Alma had never been good at washing dishes.

She sat down facing me across the table. "Well, you really did it tonight!"

I took my first bite. "It's a little cold, though," I said.

"Listen to her up there! And all over a silly thing like her inviting a perfectly nice friend home to introduce him to you. You should be ashamed of yourself! You bigot, yelling at her like that! And ordering her new friend out of the house!"

"You sure have a way with words, dear," I said.

"You're a pompous, self-centered, egotistical racist! I never should've married you. Except you had a good job, and were earning good money. However, when it comes to the way you're treating our little girl, even your career isn't compensation enough!"

"Pass the ketchup, would you, dear?" I said.

"Nope! I'm not going to let you ruin her with your stupid prejudice!"

"Yes, dear. Want some ketchup yourself?" I held up the bottle.

"You may think I'm not being serious about this, but believe me, it has come to a parting of the ways. When you can't wait before making things hard on that sweet kid, it's time for you and me to say goodbye to each other! Are you reading me on this?"

"Oh?" I looked up. "You haven't started on your dinner yet, sweetheart. It really is excellent."

"A parting of the ways," she continued. "Yes indeed. Tomorrow I'm taking her to Mother's, and you'd better change your ways before I come back!"

"You're taking a trip?" I asked. "That's nice."

"So you can just finish your dinner alone. I'm going upstairs to help Nellie pack." She left the table.

"Say hello to Mother," I called after her.

I turned to face the orangatang sitting on the barstool that was usually mine at Red's place. "So you're Osgood P. Fuggs," I said. I was more than a little sloshed, and he didn't look so big to me now, despite his gigantic arms and yard-wide shoulders. He just looked half-big.

"That's right, Jeff," he said, and extended a friendly paw.

"How'd you know my name?" I hollered.

"Farnsworth told me I'd meet you here."

I ended up in a coughing jag. "So he did, that little – !"

"He's a good fellow, Farnsworth," Fuggs said admiringly.

"You don't fool me," I lathered, leaving the barstool and poking my nose straight at his burly chest. "All you 'tangs are after is my job! And I won't let you get it!"

"After your what?"

"My job! Everybody's job! You're trying to be so damn superior, when all you are is just monkeys from the jungle! Jungle, haah! Do you hear?"

"Oh, sure, sure." Fuggs held me up with his paws under my armpits while I raspberried him in the face. "I think you've had a little too much. Come over to one of the booths with me and we'll talk."

"I don't wanna talk with no monkey! No, haah!"

Fuggs put me down. "Okay. How about me buying you another drink? Like maybe a nice hot coffee?"

"No hot coffee neither! Put up yer dukes!" I danced around him, fisticuffing. "Lemme show you who's boss!"

Red made a move to stop me, coming around the bar. Fuggs signaled that it was all right, and I saw Red smile.

"Defend yourself like a man!" I shouted, and Fuggs placed a paw on my head.

"C'mon an' fight!" I reasoned. "What's wrong with you? Ya chicken? Can't fight like a man, haah? 'Cause you ain't a man, are ya! Haah! You'se just a worthless gorilla! Haah, haah!"

The harder I swung, the harder Fuggs held my head.

"Can't hold me back, ya ape!" I yelped, getting absolutely nowhere.

Fuggs started to laugh. Not jeeringly or cruelly, but in great good humor. It amazed me to hear such a human sound coming from an orangatang. His laughing spread around the room, catching on with other customers. Two orangatangs in a far corner howled with hilarity, slapping each other.

I caught myself laughing too. Soon Fuggs and I were laughing together.

Fuggs grinned. "Say uncle?"

"Okay, Osgood," I said. "Uncle! There, I said it. Fair and square."

"Buy the loser a drink?" he proposed. I accepted.

We sat together on adjoining barstools. Red took our orders, and I turned to Fuggs.

"I never knew orangatangs could laugh."

"For your edification," he said, "it's 'orangutan,' which means 'man of the forest' in Borneo, where my people originally came from."

"You don't say," I said. "How 'bout that. So it's 'orangutan,' is it?"

He nodded. "Yup." Then he focused more closely on me. "You don't know much about us, do you?"

I gazed down at my drink. "I guess not."

Then he put a giant hand on my shoulder. "But you're learning."

I glanced across at him again. "Can you get drunk?"

He grinned. "Let's find out."

For the rest of that night I don't remember a great deal about what happened. I do remember trying to drink Fuggs under the table at each of two dozen different bars. It had never occurred to me before that I could be doing that much drinking. I remember strolling with him through the center of town, at two in the morning, singing all the old ribald songs I could remember. He didn't know any, he informed me. They didn't teach songs like that to orangatangs at Southern Orangatang University.

At one point a cop stopped us, and when he saw Fuggs, he taught him a few verses even I didn't know, and let us go on our way.

We walked until sunrise, holding each other up. I discovered that Fuggs was a very interesting person.

When I saw my house, I persuaded him to come inside. I figured Alma would be gone by now, on her way to her mother's. But just for fun I paused on the front lawn and yelled, "Wake up, everybody!"

An upstairs window opened and Alma leaned out.

She didn't see Fuggs, who by this time had gained the porch, and was holding onto one of the posts.

"I want you to meet a friend of mine!" I bellowed.

She nodded. "Oh, sure. You're waking the whole neighborhood!" She turned away from the window.

"No, really! You'll love him!"

Half an hour later, the door opened. Osgood, who had been leaning against it, fell backward into the house. Behind him, Alma said, "Who's this bum?"

Recovering his equilibrium, Osgood turned and tipped his fedora.

Alma yelped.

"Wife of mine," I said, "meet Osgood P. Fuggs, the new member of our company's board of directors, and also a good friend."

Alma was suddenly all smiles. She led Osgood into the dinette, while I followed, alone. She took his hat and coat, while I had to put mine away myself. She fixed coffee, one cup for her, and one for Osgood.

"So you're Osgood P. Fuggs," she crooned, sitting next to him and leaning sideways. I sat opposite. "Delighted to meet you."

"Same here, Missus Beemus," Osgood replied.

"My, you're a big one," she said admiringly. She felt his arm with a hand. Osgood slid away from her.

"He's our new junior executive," I repeated, just to be in on the conversation.

"Yes." Osgood was glad to change the subject. "I was lucky to land such a position. You know, Jeff, I think I'm going to like working with you."

"Thank you," I said. "You surprise me. You're really not pushy at all. Not like I thought."

"See, dear?" Alma chided. "You were all wrong, as usual. You're too narrow-minded."

Osgood came to my defense. "Now, ma'am. He's a heck of a good guy once you get to know him."

"Thank you," I said.

"You've got a great husband there, Missus Beemus," Osgood said. "He and I had a good time last night. And he showed me how to enjoy myself."

"Something you don't learn in orangatang – I mean orangutan – school," I put in, laughing.

Alma hissed. "What a bigoted remark!"

"No, he's right," Osgood corrected. "It's all a matter of getting out and mingling. He wasn't any more wrong about my people than I used to be about humans." He took another sip of coffee. "Right, Jeff?"

"Right! You just can't become accepted automatically, simply because the law says so."

Osgood nodded. "You know, you boys would have had it lots easier back in the old days if they just hadn't passed all those laws."

Alma looked at me.

"Yeah. Read about that in your history books?"

"Exactly. All about civil rights, and the riots, and the water cannons, the ghettos, the Ku Klux Klan. What a rough time you blacks must've had."

Alma looked at him.

"But we got through, remember. We finally learned the trick of just being ourselves, and we were accepted. But personally, Osgood, I never liked the word 'black.' Just call me 'American.' And I promise not to call you an 'orangatang' any longer."

Osgood grinned. "I prefer 'ape' myself."

The Old Man of San Blas

He came out of the round door looking bewildered, his steel-colored hair jutting like crazy wings on both sides of his head. He stopped, and stood searching uncertainly for a landmark.

He tried to stay balanced atop his shadow, under the hostile, bombarding sun, waiting for the sky to fall.

It didn't fall.

After waiting for several minutes, the man, wearing a baggy white suit that draped on his bones, uttered a joyous little sound in his throat and continued his journey toward the wrought-iron gate. This would be the first walk he had taken outside his house in a long time.

He opened the gate, and moved out into areas where he no longer felt that he belonged. It frightened him to think that he had no further business these days going outside into the streets of San Blas. Once, probably very long ago, he had felt much more at home in this part of Mexico.

But now it didn't seem to be his town anymore. It was populated by strangers.

All down the street, he followed the bright, whitewashed adobe wall, watching his shadow. The women and the naked children walking barefoot in the hot dust looked at him with expressions of fond appreciation. They all knew him.

He was the maker of words.

Escritor was his name among the people of the village, and he walked with as steady a gait as he could muster, pulling his bent frame to its greatest possible height. That his face was covered with a fine mat of white stubble didn't bother him, although he had once been known as a very dapper and careful person. He had once dressed finely and well, but now he no longer considered his appearance important.

He had owned the big house with the round door and the dusty courtyard for nearly a quarter of a century now, and it had slowly acquired the name Bibliotheca. It was still a grand and imposing house, but no longer a library.

For Escritor, once a lover of this land, its people, its climate, and its varied riches, hadn't written a word in twenty years, and had gradually given all his books away to the naked children. He spent too much time dreaming these days.

Ramon saw him from across the street, upstairs in a cool shadowed cave of an apartment. The old man passed just below his window as he sat at his writing table, scribbling more words into a book of his own. He was at first surprised, and then delighted to see the old man outside again, walking in the sun.

Quickly he hurried out of his apartment, and down the outdoor stairs, still in cool shadow under the building, and then he rushed out into the brilliant light, feeling the sun strike him like a firebrand on the neck as he crossed the street.

Cautiously he followed the old man, watching his faltering steps and treading in the same places. Gradually he drew up alongside, and was pacing the old man before he was noticed.

"Oh, it's you, Ramon," the old man said. "I didn't know you were still living here. Why are you still here?"

"I am working on a big fine book, Escritor, like the ones you have in your wonderful hacienda."

The old man did not interrupt his stroll, but only turned one eye to the gangling youth beside him. "A book, you say?"

"Si, yes! A big book I will want you to see!"

Escritor looked the shaggy Mexican up and down. His white clothes hung on his frame like they were hung on sticks.

"But," the old man said, suddenly concerned, "you look like you're starving! There's no meat on your bones! Do you ever eat anymore? Remember, you were once almost a glutton!"

Ramon grinned, and then frowned. Escritor had turned his attention back to his pathway along the base of the wall. He tried to draw his old friend's attention again.

"I have been writing too often to eat! And I work when I am not writing. But still I eat enough, you need not worry."

Ramon gathered his words.

"I have gone very far into my book, Escritor, very far! And it is to be the grandest of all books!"

"What is it about?" said the old man.

Ramon thought. "Everything," he finally said.

"Ah," said Escritor. "That is very good."

Ramon followed his friend across a narrow street and along the front of a church. Scents of green plants and fruits came over the adobe walls, and the running trickle of fountains.

"Ramon," said the old man, "why don't you work more, and make more money, instead of writing so much? Then at least you could eat, and maybe find a woman and marry her, and build a fine house to live in and raise a family."

Ramon tried to walk and gesture at the same time.

"You yourself said, over a year ago, Escritor, that if I could write a good big book, I should spend all my energy and all my time in its writing, until it were done, and done well. Because then, when I had the book finished, and it was a good book, I would never die, but would live forever in the book."

"Did I say that?" said Escritor.

"Yes!" said Ramon. "And also you said that if a man has written a book, he will never live alone, because there are so few who can do such things, and those who can't must warm their hands and gather close around those who can."

Escritor mused about this as he walked.

"Yes," he said quietly, "yes, I said that once."

"And – and also," Ramon went on, "you said that if a man is able to do one great thing in his life, he should do it, and forsake everything else. Because life is too short, and to die without something great having been done would be like dying sadly and alone, with nothing but bad memories and anguish."

Escritor nodded his white head. He had said that, too.

"And so, old friend," Ramon went on, "I figure that if I can finish this one big book I will have made my life worth something. And then if I were to die, it wouldn't matter, for there it would be just the same, the big, grand book I wrote."

Ramon walked with the old man.

"I want to be immortal," he said.

Pebbled and sandy, the ground crunched with their steps.

Escritor laughed gently to himself. He put an arm around the skeletal Mexican. "Come into the cantina with me, and we'll drink together."

As one, they tumbled through the doors of the cantina and into a new darkness composed of wood, and clay, and dark faces.

Very little sunlight entered this tomblike room.

A small band of nut-brown men slowly came to life in the darkness, and eyes lit up as a few hands thrust forth in recognition. "The old man, the Escritor," someone said.

"Come, come, have a drink with us!" another said.

"Ah, and Ramon, the apprentice, is with him."

Ramon was very proud of this moment.

Escritor, arm around Ramon, waved off the others. He had to regain balance and momentum, and wait for his tired eyes to adjust, before proceeding to the large, oiled bar.

And then they chose adjoining stools and sat easily, looking over the bar at themselves in the faded mirror.

Escritor felt his stubbled chin with one hand. He was getting very old. Ramon was older-looking as well.

"Cervesas!" he gestured.

Two cold glasses of beer were placed before them on the counter by the mustachioed bartender.

Escritor took his glass, and toasted Ramon's new book.

"So you want to be immortal," he said at length.

"Yes," said Ramon, putting his glass down.

"By writing a great large book about everything."

"Yes," said Ramon. "And it gets bigger by the day."

The old man took another long pull at his drink, and let its coolness fill his throbbing sunburnt brain. He leaned back, started to say something, and then decided not to.

In the silence, other conversations in the room went on.

"Well, old one," Ramon smiled, "it is certainly good to see you once again! You are looking well."

"Thank you," said Escritor.

"What have you been doing all these months inside that house? Nobody ever comes and goes from there except your housemaid, Adelita. Do you keep yourself in your library?"

Escritor, wordless, took another draught of cold beer.

"You have been working on your greatest book?" said Ramon.

"No," said Escritor.

"You have been writing poems?"

"No."

Ramon pondered a moment. Then he said, "Short stories?"

"No, Ramon," said the old man. "I have done no writing."

Ramon was mildly shocked. "But why?"

"I can't write," the old man said. "I shouldn't write."

Ramon sucked in his breath and stared at his friend. This was no kind of talk from a man like Escritor, who had grown famous in distant lands through his great books, and had brought his fame here to Mexico, and had built his marvelous Bibliotheca, and had filled it with books.

They sat silently for a long time after that, Ramon thinking on what his old friend and mentor had said. He remembered the days when he would talk long in late afternoons with Escritor, and the old man would say beautiful things about the olive trees, the avocado trees, and the endless Mexican sky. Those were glorious days for him, and the most glorious day of all had been the day that the Escritor had given him two fine books, books that the Escritor had written himself. His American name was printed on their covers. One of them was about Mexico. It was a long book which Ramon still kept carefully, and which he had read several times. The books had been made in a factory in America, and were the most beautiful he had seen.

"And you can't write either," said the old man suddenly. Ramon couldn't reconcile or believe what the old man had said.

He stared at Escritor.

"Come on, *compadre*, let's sit at a table," Escritor said.

They took their drinks from the bar and went to a table deep in the depths of the cantina.

Escritor readjusted himself after an ungainly fall which had been halted at the last second by the creaking chair.

"Let me tell you why you can't write. Why I can't write."

"I don't want to hear such talk," Ramon said into his glass.

"We can't write because it does no good."

Ramon couldn't believe that. He had a fine big book on his desk, a thousand sheets of paper bought from the bodega in Santa Ysabel, and typing on both sides of all of them, run out from his ancient typewriter which he had paid a month's wages for.

"Why do you say that, old man?"

Escritor took another sip from his glass.

"Because," he began, "what are words, anyway? I have written a million lovely words, haven't I? You have thousands of them yourself. And yet, am I any different than I was before? Am I rich? Am I famous? Do the skies open any wider for me?"

"No," said Ramon, "I guess they don't."

"Listen," said Escritor, leaning forward. "If a man builds a bridge, when he is done, there is a bridge which he and everyone can use. He can cross whatever he built the bridge to cross. And so can everyone else. The people come and see the bridge, and when they cross it, they can say, 'This is the bridge which Manuel, or Raimundo, or Cortez built!'"

"So if a man writes a book – ?" began Ramon.

"If a man writes a book, what is there to see? You cannot ride a book. You cannot eat it. You cannot wear it. It will not shield you from the rain. I have a large white house with a fine round door. And what good did all the books inside do me? I still got older. I still got drunk, and still walked in the hot sun when I went outside, just like a poor farmer with his soil gone fallow on him. I was no better.

"So I gave all my books away."

"But Escritor," said Ramon. "What of reading the books?"

"What of it? Not all the people in this world could read my books. Not even a few of them. If they could read at all, they would probably be reading in other languages. And if they could read in my own language, they'd probably be too busy. If I were to begin wasting my time reading my own books, which I wrote so long ago, it would take me an uncommon amount of time, more than I'd want to waste in reading. I would be dead before I had read them all. And what if I did read them all? Would I have really listened to myself reading? No.

"And do you know how terribly long it takes to read a book? One could build a dozen proud things in the time it take to do so. One could build empires in the time it takes to write one. I wrote hundreds of books. Have I any empires?"

"Yes!" blurted Ramon.

"Yes?" said Escritor.

"Certainly. You built great leagues of dreams in that one book you gave to me. It was about Mexico, of course, but although I have lived in Mexico all my life, I have never enjoyed living here as much as I enjoyed living in your book."

"And while you were living in the book, Ramon, were you doing anything else? Anything real and lasting?"

Ramon paused. "No, Escritor, I was reading the book."

"There, young friend, you see?" Escritor held up a hand. "Another round over here, compadre!"

More cervezas-con-frio arrived at the table.

"No, old man," said Ramon into his glass. "I don't see. I see only that you are tired, and old, and sorry for yourself. And that you have lost hope and have decided to stay poor."

"Well, young friend," said Escritor, "what else is there for a man like me to do?"

"Write one more book, Escritor! Write one for me! For our village, for Mexico! For yourself! If you are to die, Escritor, die with something left behind that will go on living!"

"You still believe that, don't you," said the old man.

"I believe that with a book written, a man need never die. His voice comes down through the ages and touches the minds and souls of countless generations to come, just as though he were still alive."

Escritor would say no more.

They finished the beer.

As Ramon got up to leave, he said, "And so I am going to write my book. And I will give it to you to read, whenever you are ready to read it."

He turned to go.

Escritor raised his head and said, "Good luck, amigo. Write a good book. And don't listen too much to an old man."

Ramon was gone.

Many days went by after that. A month went by. A year came with frost and rain, and left with a shower of leaves from the olive tree in the court of the Bibliotheca.

And Escritor, half-sober, hobbling on a leg gone newly sore, wandered among the empty shelves of his library.

He remembered his books. He tried to remember the stories. He saw the characters he had created so long ago come marching back through the open windows at night.

He saw the gallant young man fighting to hold a canyon in 1939, during the Revolution.

He saw the tender young soldier tormented by venereal disease trying to appreciate a goddess of a nurse while he lay dying in a sanitarium. He himself standing on a high mountainside in Sonora.

He saw all the spring days, all the summer nights, all the whistling winters of his youth.

And though he thought he had forgotten, he hadn't.

And one morning, Escritor saw the manuscript. Adelita, who had cleaned the house for him, and brought his food, had placed it on the big oak table in the library. It was a gigantic heap of papers, stapled, tied with strings, and clipped with paperclips.

It was Ramon's book.

Escritor went over to it, and looked at it for a long while before picking it up. An old respect and exhilaration filtered through his consciousness as he laid a hand on top of it.

Here was a book, a real book, which had been written clear through to the end.

Ramon had been writing very much indeed.

Escritor found himself caught up in the excitement of the moment. He forgot his dreamings and took part of the huge manuscript and went over to a chair, to sit down and read it.

Here was a tangible thing, a palpable thing, a creation of typewritten words, which could be read and pondered at leisure, a drama of characters and moods and motivations, all run out on paper, ready to be read by anyone who cared to take the time.

The old feelings were seeping into Escritor's dulled mind. Feelings of pride and envy combined, what he had always felt when holding a manuscript he hadn't written himself, which he had never expected to feel so solidly in his hands.

Sitting down in a chair, he began reading.

The world of the book flowed out off the pages and filled his entire being with new visions.

Escritor didn't eat the dinner Adelita brought into the room with mothering comments. He went on reading Ramon's book. He didn't sleep that night, but continued reading. All through the following day he was back at the oak table for new chapters. The story had a grip on him now, as his permanent hangover melted away under a new stimulation.

He spent four days reading the book.

And when he was through to the last page, he laid it on his knees where he sat, and smiled to himself.

It was a good book. A great book.

Ramon had proven his point.

The next morning, after a long night's restful sleep, Escritor found a note by his bedside, where he had placed Ramon's manuscript. Adelita had left it there. It was from Ramon.

Escritor stood at the bedroom window, and read the note.

"Good morning, old friend," it began. "I hope that by now you have had time to take a look at my book. If you have read it clear through, as I hope you have, then I hope you liked it. And also, I feel that if you have indeed read it through, now is the time to tell you why I wrote so much into a single book. It is because that one book is all I will ever write. I have a disease of the bones, and have known for years that I must die from it. And now, very close to the end, I am sure that I finished the book just in time. I believe that when you read this note I will have already died. If that is so, then, dear friend, remember me by my book. Think of the book as myself, able to live forever. And, please, take care of the book for me. It, and myself as well, are in your hands. In death as in life, your amigo, Ramon."

Escritor put the note into his pocket. He turned to look again at the manuscript. He looked at his hands, and turned them over.

And then he rushed out of the room, down the stairs, and out of the round door. When, in the courtyard, the sun struck him on the back of the neck he rushed toward the gate, and gripped the iron bars with his hands. He looked out into the brilliant-white street. Something cold surged through him.

The air was uncommonly quiet today. And across the street a crowd of people wearing black were gathered. A doctor was there.

And down from Ramon's apartment they were carrying a thin, unbelievably insubstantial form on a pallet, draped in white.

Escritor pushed open the gate, and stumbled across the dusty street. He forced his way violently through the gathering of old women, children and young men milling around the base of the shadowed stairway on which was being borne the strange white pallet.

"Who is it?" he roared into the cool shadow.

Faces turned and stared at the old man.

A few lit up in recognition. "It is the Escritor," said a nut-brown girl with long jet-black braids.

The white pallet, covered with a sheet, was brought before the old man, the Escritor.

"It is Ramon," said one of the bearers.

"He is dead," said another.

"He died in the night," said the doctor, "in his sleep."

Escritor stood for a long time in the brilliant sun while the white pallet was placed on shoulders, with a great deal of ceremony, while old women chewed tangerines, and children played with their clothes, fidgeting.

When the little sad procession had gone up the hill toward the church, Escritor turned and went back into his big house.

Ramon's manuscript squatted solidly on the oak table.

Escritor took it carefully and carried it into his writing room, where a rusting typewriter was gathering cobwebs on a massive, hand-carved mahogany desk.

He knew Ramon had been right.

He knew what had to be done now.

Escritor sat at the aging machine, and touched the keys. He inserted paper, and began to type.

He hadn't used the machine in a great many years, and for a long moment, he tried to regain his old skill. Slowly, the touch returned. The feel of the keys was an old comfort.

He started writing in earnest.

This was to be a glorious epitaph to Ramon, and the beginning of a legend. A book by a half-man, half-boy whom nobody had ever known but him. But all the same, Ramon had just been reborn in the book and would grow anew to unexpected stature, and might possibly live forever.

Escritor felt old and now-familiar pains in his own body. He felt the insistent knock of Death at his door. He felt the vast weight of all he hadn't done bearing down on him.

While he worked the typewriter, he thought of the greatness he would make of Ramon's book. Of the final copies he would send to his old publisher in New York.

He also thought, in the back of his mind, of a final book he himself must write. A book about a small Mexican who had changed his life just in time to save it forever.

Escritor felt a new energy in him. A new yearning.

With renewed strength, he fell fully to his work.

Afterword:
The Story of this Book

This book wasn't even a dream before the end of 1969.

I'd decided to try being a writer in 1961 (the exact time was the evening of January 7, though this is hardly important, and may not even be accurate). I'd been reading stories by Robert Sheckley, Arthur C. Clarke, and Ray Bradbury. And I'd just found a copy of L. Sprague de Camp's *Science Fiction Handbook* at the local public library.

It was de Camp who showed me that it was possible not just to read SF but to actually write it, and perhaps even *sell* it and have it published! The thought of such sheer possibility had gone straight to my head.

I was fifteen years old at the time, and would be turning sixteen in another two months (the end of March). So I set myself a deadline. I would sell a story to one of the magazines listed in the back of de Camp's book by March 29!

I borrowed my grandmother's Smith-Corona portable typewriter and got started at once, writing a tale about an astronaut (or maybe "time-o-naut") being sent by a giant government time-travel program into the future.

He goes there, and climbs out of his capsule to find himself indoors, somewhere in a vast beehive world of rooms whose occupants can see and do just about everything they want, as long as it's in the virtual world of their small, isolated rooms.

189

But there's a problem. The future-man whose room our time traveler has invaded has never heard of time travel, which he insists is impossible. And he's never heard anything else about the time traveler's past. Finally the time traveler returns to his capsule, looks at his gauges, and learns the incredible truth. He's hit some sort of barrier and has rebounded the other way, ending up nearly a billion years in the past.

(If you've looked at the other tales in this book, you no doubt will recognize this plot. I've reconstructed it from memory, since the original manuscript is long since lost, and include it here as "Intruder.")

It took me about a year to realize I was laboring under a major delusion. L. Sprague de Camp had published his *Handbook* in 1953, at the apex of the postwar, post-atomic science fiction boom, when there had been about 40 monthly magazines buying stories. But now, eight years later, the boom was over and the magazines were gone.

I kept getting those early stories back, usually with "addressee unknown" stamped, or written, on the envelopes.

By the autumn of 1962 I'd given up trying to publish my stories. I switched to writing new ones only for myself, binding them into small "magazines" with covers I designed. I stored these away and got them out occasionally to look at them again.

Having found myself alone in the outside world, I'd turned inward.

But I didn't stop writing.

At the same time, much earlier in 1962, I found a way that I could meet Ray Bradbury. Before leaving L. A. High, where I'd been going to school, I contacted him and managed to arrange for him to come to the school he'd attended himself 25 years earlier, to give a talk to as many of the students as I could persuade to show up.

That event was more successful than I ever expected it to be. The hall which the school provided was packed with about 500 people. I took the podium and introduced Bradbury, after which he proceeded to hold them spellbound, or so it seemed, for the following two hours. Nobody got up to leave. Nobody fidgeted, or talked, or acted nervous. Bradbury held them in his hands until he finished speaking.

Afterward I asked him if I could see him again, and he invited me to his Beverly Hills office...and to bring along some of my stories.

What followed were two years of excitement, not just for me but for my entire family: me, my younger brother, my divorced mother, and my grandmother.

Bradbury sent us tickets to a presentation of three of his stories that he'd rewritten as one-act plays. He arranged for me to appear on camera when David Wolper (who would later produce the only financially successful Olympiad in the history of the Olympics, the 1984 games in Los Angeles) filmed a half-hour episode about him for his television series *Story of a Writer*. They showed me climbing the stairs, a blond-haired, chubby teenager with one of my self-published magazines in my hand.

And he invited me to the Pacific Coast Writers' Conference at L. A. State College, where he introduced me to Leon Surmelian, who had organized the conference, and to *Twilight Zone* screenwriter Charles Beaumont.

Therein hangs another tale. Beaumont turned out to be much older than I'd expected him to be, considering the youthfulness and inventiveness of his stories (I'd found his paperback *The Hunger* at the local newsstand where I was buying most of my paperbacks at the time). He was a little, shriveled, wizened, gray-haired elf with a hideously wrinkled face and gnarly, bony hands. I hesitated to shake his hand, for fear that his would crumble into dust at my touch.

It wasn't until almost thirty years later, in the '90s, that I would learn that Beaumont had actually only been in his thirties when I'd met him! He was suffering from a severe, terminal case of premature aging. In another year, in fact, he would be dead.

By 1970, however, Bradbury and I had drifted apart.

I got a job, bought my first car (he has always hated automobiles), began smoking (he has also hated cigarettes, for good reason!), and discovered that I could sell more stories to the newly burgeoning "adult" magazines, imitations of *Playboy*, than I could've ever hoped to sell to the SF pulps...and for more money, too!

During those years I peddled encyclopedias, vacuum cleaners, and educational materials door to door all over southern California, worked as a typesetter at a commercial printing company, wrote and sold three novels (what Fat Freddy of Gilbert Shelton's "Fabulous Furry Freak

Brothers" was calling fuck books), and ended up drawing a series of comic strips for the newsboys at the Hollywood *Citizen-News*, working in my own storefront office.

In 1962 my mother had bought her own house, at last, in the idyllic suburbs of the San Fernando Valley, and my brother and I had finally moved out of the giant, rambling, two-story bungalow in downtown L.A. which belonged to my grandmother, where I'd been growing up.

The Valley in the early '60s was like heaven, with tree-shaded streets, backyard swimming pools (I'd never imagined such luxury!) and neighbors who included a successful electronic engineer, a media consultant, an architect and a Dutch baron whose paintings had appeared several times on the covers of *The Reader's Digest.*

I became part of this community for the next twelve years, while I studied architecture on my own, bought a reel-to-reel tape recorder and a stereo system, and began amassing a library of recordings, and continued to write novels and stories.

Then, one day in 1969, I found a new paperback book on a display rack at a neighborhood bookstore which, when I checked the copyright page, turned out to have been published by a company whose offices were only a few blocks from my house!

In only a few hours I'd gone there. The publisher himself met me and we shook hands. His name was Bill Trotter, he was from Chicago, and had been a paperback distributor for the past several years. I told him that I was a published writer, with several story sales and three novels to my credit. He was impressed. It didn't matter that most of what I'd sold had been in the new sexual-revolution vein of writing (not exactly what would pass for pornography these days, but certainly far beyond what anyone had seen, or read, before then). He asked me to put together a SF anthology as soon as I could...because he needed something to publish!

Only about a week later I was back with a pile of my old manuscripts. I'd retyped much of it. I'd also reconstructed a number of my early stories that had been lost. Bill handed them over to a girl named Kathleen Galbraith, a young blonde he'd recently hired to be his first book editor, and she began to oversee transforming this rough material into a book.

By the beginning of 1970 *Santana Morning* came out. It was my first *legitimate* foray into publication, and I'll never forget the joy I felt when I held one of those first copies in my hands.

But the fate of that original edition ended up being a sad one.

William Powell Trotter might've been an experienced book distributor. But he was not a book *publisher*.

As soon as Forrey Ackerman heard about Powell Publications, he offered to supply Bill with as many ready-made paperback books as he could manage. Unfortunately these were leftover projects that had been done in a much different style many years earlier, from writers Forrey had been representing since the 1930s, whose stories had originally appeared in *Famous Fantastic Mysteries, Thrilling Wonder Stories*, and *Weird Tales*. Forrey even provided the covers.

Trotter let Ackerman go ahead with these efforts, and they began coming out with the Powell label. But they were not Powell books.

At the same time Galbraith was also working with other writers and bringing out such books as Charles Fritch's *Crazy Mixed-Up Planet* and *Horses' Asteroid*, and Don Wollheim's *Two Dozen Dragon Eggs*, with covers by Bill Hughes of New Mexico, whose art also graced the cover of *Santana Morning*.

But Kable News Company, the distributor Powell had found, had changed their specialty and was focusing on the ballooning adult-bookstore trade, and copies of all his paperbacks started showing up alongside the fuck books and underground comics that all such stores were selling, along with offering peepshows in the back, and dildoes and other sex toys up front.

Because of this, nobody who wanted to read SF or fantasy even got a chance to see a Powell book. And the people who wanted sex thrills were bound to be disappointed when they found only stories about spaceships or haunted houses instead.

And so, as Bill told me sadly, the day after he'd declared bankruptcy, about a million copies of Powell's books, including several thousand of *Santana Morning*, had been stripped of their covers and consigned to landfills, to be reassimilated into Planet Earth's ecology.

Thus ended Powell, and my hopes for this collection of stories, and my career as a SF and fantasy writer for the foreseeable future.

193

By 1974 I'd moved out of Los Angeles for good and was building a house for myself and my mother (who was paying for it) in Colorado.

I went to work writing a humor column and reporting, for *The Mountain Mail* in Salida. Later I found a woman in New Jersey who was publishing several sex-advice magazines (the current form that adult fiction had taken in the early 1980s). She bought more than a hundred stories from me, all extremely short, and published them anonymously...but paid me on time, with checks that didn't bounce.

And I continued writing. I succeeded in fooling my editor and publisher at *The Mountain Mail* into printing a number of new short stories, disguised as installments of "On the Flip Side." One of these, "The Truth about the Elves" would win an award for the paper from the Colorado Press Association, for best feature by a weekly newspaper.

More than a year ago, at age 60, on the verge of turning 61, I discovered something amazing. I got an e-mail from someone who had found a battered copy of *Santana Morning* years earlier, in a dusty cardboard box in the back of a small store in an isolated town in South Carolina. And, in his message to me, he said that the stories he'd read in that book, my book, had inspired him to become prolific, successful ambient-music composer!

This reminds me of how I first found many of Sheckley's, Clarke's, and Bradbury's books. I'd been snooping, aimlessly, through some old cartons of junk in a store on Western Avenue in Los Angeles, in the summer of 1959, and had found dozens of Ballantine paperbacks that someone had evidently thrown out. I'd asked the guy how much he wanted for them, and he'd startled me by saying, "Gimme a dollar and you can take the whole box."

That afternoon I'd walked home with my head in the clouds and an entire *library* of SF and fantasy in my arms!

The world is a strange place, I've learned. Stranger, perhaps, and more wondrous, than anybody could imagine. Strings of cause-and-effect stretch out through wildernesses of misdirection and coincidence, and suddenly, after decades, one of those you'd utterly given up on suddenly snaps you back with a connection to something utterly unexpected!

That was what happened to me. My old paperback anthology, this book here, reached out through someone I'd never even met and hauled me back into a world I'd assumed for most of my life was totally lost. And this strand, this thread, this tenuous spiderweb filament of happenstance and serendipity, linked me to a reader I'd never thought was out there.

At the same time, I heard through his daughter Zee (Alexandra), that Ray Bradbury himself had learned of the ongoing existence of my old anthology. Later, Zee relayed a message from Ray in which he congratulated me on the book's possible restoration and rebirth.

And so at long last, here is the book again, and the stories, plus others I've added. Read them, copy them, hold onto them if you want, and pass them along. I never expected them to live again, but here they are, still breathing and kicking, even after lying for more than 35 years in their graves.

Mike Dolan
Buena Vista, Colorado,
November 29, 2007

More quality fiction from Elastic Press

☐	The Virtual Menagerie	Andrew Hook	SOLD OUT
☐	Open The Box	Andrew Humphrey	SOLD OUT
☐	Second Contact	Gary Couzens	SOLD OUT
☐	Sleepwalkers	Marion Arnott	SOLD OUT
☐	Milo & I	Antony Mann	SOLD OUT
☐	The Alsiso Project	Edited by Andrew Hook	SOLD OUT
☐	Jung's People	Kay Green	SOLD OUT
☐	The Sound of White Ants	Brian Howell	SOLD OUT
☐	Somnambulists	Allen Ashley	SOLD OUT
☐	Angel Road	Steven Savile	SOLD OUT
☐	Visits to the Flea Circus	Nick Jackson	SOLD OUT
☐	The Elastic Book of Numbers	Edited by Allen Ashley	SOLD OUT
☐	The Life To Come	Tim Lees	SOLD OUT
☐	Trailer Park Fairy Tales	Matt Dinniman	SOLD OUT
☐	The English Soil Society	Tim Nickels	£5.99
☐	The Last Days of Johnny North	David Swann	SOLD OUT
☐	The Ephemera	Neil Williamson	SOLD OUT
☐	Unbecoming	Mike O'Driscoll	£6.99
☐	Photocopies of Heaven	Maurice Suckling	SOLD OUT
☐	Extended Play	Edited by Gary Couzens	£6.99
☐	So Far, So Near	Mat Coward	£5.99
☐	Going Back	Tony Richards	£5.99
☐	That's Entertainment	Robert Neilson	£5.99
☐	The Cusp of Something	Jai Clare	£5.99
☐	Other Voices	Andrew Humphrey	£5.99
☐	Another Santana Morning	Mike Dolan	£5.99
☐	Binding Energy	Daniel Marcus	£5.99

All these books are available at your local bookshop or can be ordered direct from the publisher. Indicate the number of copies required and fill in the form below.

Name_____
(Block letters please)

Address_____

Send to Elastic Press, 85 Gertrude Road, Norwich, Norfolk, NR3 4SG.
Please enclose remittance to the value of the cover price plus: £1.50 for the first book plus 50p per copy for each additional book ordered to cover postage and packing. Applicable in the UK only.

While every effort is made to keep prices low, it is sometimes necessary to increase prices at short notice. Elastic Press reserve the right to show on covers and charge new retail prices which may differ from those advertised in the text or elsewhere.

Want to be kept informed? Keep up to date with Elastic Press titles by writing to the above address, or by visiting www.elasticpress.com and adding your email details to our online mailing list.

Elastic Press: Winner of the British Fantasy Society Best Small Press award 2005

Previously from Elastic Press

Other Voices by Andrew Humphrey

Andrew Humphrey follows up his acclaimed first collection, "Open The Box", with another twelve stories of loss and abandonment, fear and greed. Moving through the genres of urban horror, science fiction, crime and slipstream, Humphrey examines the effects of the fantastic upon the personal, whether through future dystopias, a missing child, climatic change, or repeated infidelity.

An original and unique vision – Eric Brown

Out Now from Elastic Press

Binding Energy by Daniel Marcus

Marcus maps out possible futures and theoretical pasts, crisscrossing reality with fantasy, and weaving intricate storylines in the process. His characters are frightened and fragile, facing brave new worlds whilst retaining their humanity. If you want to know what the future really looks like, then look here.

This is Science Fiction of the highest level. The stores ring with authenticity. The language is sharp and funny and unflinching. The science crackles – Michael Blumlein, World Fantasy Award finalist

For further information visit:
www.elasticpress.com

Forthcoming from Elastic Press

The Last Reef by Gareth L Powell

Gareth L Powell's first collection of short stories is stuffed with mind-bending ideas and unforgettable characters. Ranging from the day after tomorrow to the far-flung future, these fifteen stories are perfect for anyone with a craving for intelligent and thought-provoking adventure. From noir-ish cops to disaffected space pilots, blind photographers and low-life hackers, everyone here is struggling to find a little peace amid the tumult of the future.

With an introduction from Interzone co-editor, Jetse De Vries.

Forthcoming from Elastic Press

The Turing Test by Chris Beckett

These fourteen stories, among other things, contain robots, alien planets, genetic manipulation and virtual reality, but their centre focuses on individuals rather than technology, and how they deal with love and loneliness, authenticity, reality and what it really means to be human.

With an introduction from Alistair Reynolds.

For further information visit:
www.elasticpress.com